I0567385

The Best of CaféLit 6

The Best of CaféLit 6

an anthology

Edited by Gill James

Chapeltown Books

This collection copyright © Chapeltown Books 2017.
Copyright in the text reproduced herein remains the
property of the individual authors, and permission to
publish is gratefully acknowledged by the editors and
publishers.

All rights reserved

No parts of this publication may be reproduced, stored in a
retrieval system, or transmitted in any form or by any means,
electronic, mechanical, photocopying, recording or
otherwise without prior permission of the copyright owner.

British Library Cataloguing in Publication Data

A Record of this Publication is available from the British
Library

ISBN 978-1-910542-17-0

This edition published 2017 by Chapeltown Books
Manchester, England

All Chapeltown books are published on paper derived from
sustainable resources.

Contents

Foreword

As ever it is a delight to make the selection for the annual 'Best of'. This involves reading every single story that has been published on the web site throughout the previous year. This time we've had a few writers who have more than one story in the collection. It's revealing to see how their CVs have changed over the year. We're using the latest version.

Is there a common trait amongst these stories? Well judging by the variety of the accompanying drinks on offer, and given that the story should match the mood that the drink invokes, there must be variety in the stories too. But yes, most certainly, they all have in common that they will be good company if you stop for a drink in a café. Yet they remain diverse enough to make you smile, make you laugh, make you think or make you cry.

We're going to take a writing workshop to a couple of festivals in 2017, precisely to help people to write for CaféLit. Watch out for news on the web site: **www.cafelit.co.uk**

We are as ever always on the lookout for more writers, so if you've not had a go yet, why not submit to us? Take a look at our submission guidelines on our site: **www.cafelit.co.uk/index.php/submission-guidelines-2**

We're speeding ahead as well with flash

collections. Several are out already and some are coming out soon:
www.chapeltownpublishing.uk/p/submissions.html

CaféLit supports the work of the Creative Café Project. Half of the profit from the books is shared by authors and the other half goes into the Project. The Creative Café Project is about identifying and supporting cafés which provide a space where creative practitioners can interact with their audiences and peers. Take a look here:
www.creativecafeproject.org

Gill James

Ephemeral
Angela Haffenden

Hot cocoa with mint

Where warmth and cold collide, I exist. I am ice crystals, flakes, shimmering and falling. I silently glisten on the land, in a pure white covering. Little robin red breast leaves footprints while he searches for food. Children play; making angels, throwing balls, building snowmen with carrot noses, coal for eyes, fallen branches for arms. When the temperature rises, I melt, and slide in slabs from rooftops. Once new and fluffy and full of promise I become black and sludgy. My time on earth is over. I end my time soaking into the ground, nourishing the roots of new life.

About the Author
Angela Haffenden is a mother of four children. She is also responsible for a husband and a dog. She writes mainly to stay sane. She lives by the sea and writes in a cabin in the garden.

Pressing the Flesh
Allison Symes

Iced tea

It was 3 a.m. The neighbours were sleeping. He must be quick. It was hard to disguise a cutter's sound but bodies didn't dispose of themselves. His ancestors knew that. They provided bodies for vivisection - animal or human, it didn't matter which. There were discoveries to be made. Science then was a hungry beast.

His market was different. So many could not afford the disgusting price of meat. So many could not afford to ask where cheap meat originated and instead were sensible and just ate what they could get.

About the Author
Allison Symes is published by CaféLit, Bridge House Publishing, Chapeltown Books, Alfie Dog Fiction, Scriggler.com and Shortbread Short Stories. She is a member of the Society of Authors and Association of Christian Writers. Her website is
www.fairytaleswithbite.weebly.com

She blogs for Chandler's Ford Today
http://chandlersfordtoday.co.uk/author/allison-symes/

Pirate Island

Lloyd Jenkinson

A cup of Earl Grey Tea – light and refreshing

The boat rocked violently from side to side as the storm grew stronger.

The waves crashed on the deck and they were getting louder.

'I get in the cabin, Grandpa!' he shouted as he was thrown from side to side in the flimsy boat. His tiny fingers gripped tightly onto the sides for fear of being thrown overboard into the mouths of the waiting sharks.

'I in the cabin now!' he shouted.

We saw the beacon of a distant lighthouse in the early morning gloom. It was Pirate Island. The winds dropped as we sailed towards the flickering light and beached the boat upon the shore. It had been a terrifying journey, as I watched his little legs struggle to carry him safely through the surf.

'I found a cave, Grandpa,' he said and disappeared inside. 'Can I have torch?' he said, 'It a bit too dark in here.'

The cave was hot and sticky and we went in deeper and deeper, crawling through narrow channels, the light of his torch leading the way. As we did we heard the thump of heavy feet and felt the thud of each step. 'I no like Trolls, Grandpa,' he said, 'they scare me.'

'They're only pretend,' I said 'They're not real.'

'I still no like Trolls. No more Trolls.'

And he hit me.

'Come on Joseph, it's time to get up. Time for breakfast,' his mother said as she peered through the bedroom door.

'I not finished playing with Grandpa. We playing boats,' he shouted as he popped up from beneath the duvet and slapped the bed. 'We go to Pirate Island don't we Grandpa?'

What do you say? Support your grandson who is having fun or your daughter who wants to start the day?

'Maybe one more time?' I said.

'Okay, only one more time,' she said, 'I've got work today.'

'Come on Grandpa, make the boat again,' he said pulling up the duvet. I curved my legs and he jumped in the gap between them and started to sway one way then the other. 'Faster, Grandpa, faster.'

I made the sound of wind and waves as I rocked him from side to side. I spun the torch in my hand, like the flashing beacon of a light house. Red, then green, then white.

'I get in the cabin!' he shouted and pulled the bedspread over his head.

'No more sharks, Grandpa. I don't like sharks. You pinch me. It hurts'

'Okay, no more sharks but this is the last time.'

14

'Come on you two, breakfast is ready. Mummy's got to go to work,' said my daughter standing at the door, clinging onto a bleary-eyed sister, untimely ripped from her slumber and not yet vocal. 'Come on Grandpa, enough's enough.'

'Ookay,' I said as I stopped rocking. 'Breakfast now then, Joseph.'

Just as I thought everything was going well he shouted, 'I not hungry. I not want breakfast. Again, Grandpa, again.' He buried himself beneath the covers. His sister had now woken up and joined in. She screamed as loud as she could, her lungs almost popping out. A piercing sound showing she meant business. 'I want milk, now.'

It was strange how the high pitched whine of a distressed baby turned the volume control up in everyone. It always did.

'Now look you've upset Eleanor. Come on, breakfast is ready and Mummy has to go to work,' shouted my daughter.

It was no use as he was already at sea again, in his cabin, battling the storms. Pirate Island, sharks, sorry, they had gone by request just like the trolls, and a dark cave on a distant shore.

Where would you want to be?

About the Author
Lloyd Jenkinson is a retired surgeon who now has the time to enjoy the delights of new life and word craft.

Bite Marks

Janet Bunce

Bloody Mary – chilled

There was no doubting the marks on the body.

Teeth to be sure.

Some learned locals said they were from a wolf.

Another said a bat or maybe a large dog.

Whatever the source there was great discomfort in the village.

Years ago there had been a number of attacks.

Several had died from bite wounds, torn apart around the neck.

Rumours prevailed about a vampire but then it all suddenly stopped.

It was just a rabid dog they then concluded.

What they had not remembered was the visiting freak circus – back again and amongst its performers Countess Marie Dracula.

About the Author
Janet Bunce works in financial services but loves writing and hopes to achieve more in 2017. She is very pleased with her inclusion in the last two editions of *Best of CaféLit* and now this one.

The Queen's Labour

Dawn Knox

Mead

'The head is visible, your majesty.'

No one breathed as she paused to summon sufficient strength for the final push. Unspoken questions hung in the suffocating air of the lying-in chamber.

Was the baby alive?

Strong?

A boy?

Her destiny depended on this child. A healthy son would guarantee her status and, if not the king's love, then at least his respect. But if not…

She prayed to the Virgin Mary as she pushed, and the infant slithered, screaming into eager hands.

It was done.

Eyes avoided her gaze and expressions froze.

'Congratulations, your majesty, you have a fine daughter.'

About the Author

Dawn's second book *The Great War, 100 stories of 100 words honouring those who lived and died 100 years ago* was published in 2016. She enjoys a writing challenge and has had stories published in various anthologies, including horror and speculative fiction, as well as romances in several women's magazines. Dawn has written a script for a play to commemorate World War One, which has been performed in her home town in Essex, as well as in Germany and France. Married with one son, she lives in Essex.

Confessional

Hannah Constance

Red wine

I cannot complain, Lord. There's something so human about being inside here. Sightless, warm... a bit cramped, but nothing on earth is perfect. Just her voice ringing through the crack...

But Lord, let this ordeal be short. Or at least shorter than the last time, when I was squatting in a puddle of my own urine. But we all have to endure this time on earth. The true reward lies in Heaven.

But Lord... his voice does grind through me like a saw. I know Jesus commands that I must love, but some are more difficult to care for than others. Face like a strutting bull. A reckless, tatty way of dressing which would only be fit in a brothel, half way through a session with a courtesan. And that funny shade of purple his face turns as he yells 'Where is he? Where is he, you devil woman?' I have only the tiniest crack to see from, and I can still spy that blistering shade of purple on his cheeks.

She says nothing. I spot the hem of her dress sliding across an ankle. She knows the Lord blessed her with a calming silence and a level gaze, and now she uses these gifts to their fullest. She has always been so god-fearing, so obedient.

'Do you think I am stupid, Anne? You think I

can't smell him? A man like that... has a very distinctive stench.' I hear the sound of thumping footsteps as he roams around the room, a heaving boar trying to smell out his rival.

Finally, she speaks; a smooth, mild voice. 'I don't know what you are talking about, John.'

'Don't play your games with me! I know!'

A crash. I flinch and scuttle back further into my darkness. Did he knock things off the mantelpiece? Flip the table? I bring a nervous eye back to the crack and see only her ankle again. She hasn't moved an inch.

Her, once again: 'I don't know what you're talking about, John.'

A strange pause. Then his voice, quieter. 'I can't believe this. You don't know what I'm talking about? Just look at yourself, Anne. You're covered in proof.' A flash of an arm as he gestures at her. 'I didn't get you that necklace, did I?'

She is motionless.

'Look at it... That gold. Those jewels... It's not a subtle crucifix, Anne! A mysterious, out of the blue object that says so much about you!'

I try to angle myself to see her clearer, but I cannot see the necklace.

In her own time, she responds. 'No John. You didn't get this for me—'

'Ha!'

'Because I got it for myself.'

Another smash. I guess it to be a water jug.

'Liar!' he shouts. 'He gave it to you! And with it a direct passage to hell!'

People are taken in by the silliest things, Lord. To think Anne would go to hell for all this! People do not know real sin when they see it, Lord. Instead they thrust blame on the persecuted without a second thought. It keeps their own soul clean, they think. And as I sit here, Lord, in this humble darkness, I know true modesty. As I sit here in humble darkness, Lord, I peek out at the cruel, blinding beacon of his sin.

Her tone changes suddenly. 'I will not go to hell.'

He thumps something hard, rage building. 'Well then to jail, at least. You know the law, Anne. And you're a fool. We don't even need to find him. That crucifix can be evidence enough nowadays…'

The ankle twitches and she stands. I tense, watching. Oh Lord, stop this. Stop this sickening persecutor. I place a hand on the dark wall of my hovel and pray for her safety.

'Alright John,' she says. 'Would you like to know the truth? How I got this necklace? It was given to me by my lover.'

This silence is not like the other silences. It is deep and asphyxiating.

'Really, Anne?' his voice now whimpers. 'A lover? I didn't… I thought you had…'

'I know what you thought I had,' Anne is stern. 'I

know what you were insinuating, John. It was very clear. So let me make this clear. I got this from my lover. I did not get it from a Priest.'

He stumbles. 'But… a lover! What about us, Anne? Seven years! Anne… why? Why?'

'Because you treat me like this.'

Another silence. Then, tiny clattering noises – the apologetic sounds one makes when they are trying to tidy up the mess they have so recently made.

I see her arms crossed over her chest, crumpling the green material of her dress. Her voice grows in power. 'Once you've picked them up, I'd like you to go.'

His anger flares again and I see his body sidle up to hers. 'So you weren't a Catholic after all, Anne. Turns out you were just a tart.'

She doesn't move an inch. 'Go.'

The bull canters away. As soon as his footsteps disappear, she sinks back into her chair for a moment, head in her hands.

'Safe now, I presume?' I say, after a moment.

'Oh, yes.' She jumps up, crouches into the empty fireplace and removes the fake panel from the back. I tumble out of the priest hole, covered in soot.

'Thank you,' I say, patting down my robes.

'I take it you heard all of it,' she says, going back to her chair. 'My… marriage is over, Father.'

I touch her crucifix gently. 'But better than execution, my dear.'

She lets me sit beside her as she brushes down my robes, wiping away the last of the soot. 'Well,' she murmurs. 'It's a small price to pay really.'

'Small indeed,' I agree. 'We both know our true reward lies in Heaven.'

A pause. Anne leans over and squeezes my thigh. 'Yes… Mostly,' she says.

'Mostly, Anne.' I touch her breast.

About the author
Hannah Constance is a Drama and Creative Writing graduate from Salford University. Her prose can be found in *The Askance 2014 Short Story Collection, Homes.*

Performance

Roger Noons

A glass of rosé

The unwanted McDonalds remains surely contained a beacon, for within seconds of being casually dropped on the crossing, the scavengers homed in.

A black-backed gull strutted from stage right: a rook catapulted in from the left and two magpies occupied centre stage. Undirected, seemingly unrehearsed, devoid of floodlights, watched by a select audience confined within a blue four by four Kia, the improvised black and white ballet unfolded.

Accompanied by *kyows, chak-chaks and kaws*, monogrammed paper was shredded, morsels of food tossed, juggled, grabbed and devoured until, the stage bare, the performers exited as if wired in audition for pantomime.

About the Author
Roger Noons is a regular contributor to CaféLit, wowing us with many 100 worders and some longer ones – and you can also read his stories in our *Best of CaféLit* series.

Poppy, a Puppy for Remembrance
Linda Flynn

Tia Maria

She was not born on Remembrance Day, although I remember the day quite clearly. It was the day that Bill died.

His six closest friends and family traipsed into his cottage in a mournful procession, but by that stage he could hardly speak. It had seemed strange to me that we weren't greeted by his black Labrador, Tia. But then dogs have their own way of grieving. The two of them had been inseparable as she followed him like his sleek, silent shadow.

I leant over Bill's rasping body, wrapped in a crocheted bedspread. Shakily he gestured to his bedside table and I picked up a crumbling cardboard box. Gingerly I lifted the lid to reveal three war medals. He made some guttural sounds, mouthed repeatedly. I strained my ear towards him, but I could not decipher what it was that he was trying to say.

I moved back and gave an anxious look to Simon, his son, but he just gave a bewildered shrug.

It was his granddaughter who first heard them. A strange, high pitched yelping.

As Bill drew his last breath the sound became louder, more insistent.

We all stood still with our heads bowed in respect,

too overwhelmed to register anything beyond that moment.

Outside a field of poppies stirred in the gentle June breeze. I imagined Bill's soul slipping through the corn field, brushing against the crimson petals and then taking flight.

I felt a small, insistent tug on my arm and I looked into the large olive eyes of Bill's great granddaughter, Maria. 'Come to the kitchen,' she whispered.

We heard the little whimpers before even the door was open. There on the hearth lay Tia, surrounded by six sausage-like puppies wriggling and writhing.

So it was that we each received a puppy for remembrance, with Bill's son also keeping Tia. I decided to call my lively little black puppy, with her twitching inquisitive nose, Poppy.

Now a year on, I return to walk through Bill's field once again. I park my car in a nearby lay by, then we cautiously cross the busy road. Bill used to complain at the road kill, when reckless drivers regularly ran over birds, rabbits, even a deer.

Poppy is tumbling ahead of me, twirling through the corn. I call her back and she hurtles towards me, her tail thumping.

My fingers sink into her soft fur and I gently rub her chin. She nuzzles closer, her toffee eyes beseeching me for more.

Then off she bounds again; leaping like a deer over strands of corn, sniffing unusual smells and jumping backwards at the whirring of a pheasant's wings.

I think of Bill's rheumy grey eyes and soft smile. I used to listen for hours to his tales of endurance in battle, wrapped up as stories. Yet each time he heard an explosion: a car exhaust, a champagne cork or even the popping of some logs on his fire, and he would flinch, turning into himself. His eyes would stare intently forward, his body rigid. Tia would lean her wise head on his lap and wait patiently. I would creep away, afraid to disturb his silent reverie.

Now he has given me a puppy to look after and who also cared for me. It was Poppy who helped me through when I dealt with the wrenching cramp like pain of divorce. As I felt the door slam on my past, she would nuzzle her damp nose on to my lap and lift her soft padded paws over me. I found comfort in leaning my head against her gentle warm fur, knowing that she would never desert me.

Then there was the night of the burglary. Poppy had alerted me with her feverish barking, but they had still managed to steal all of Bill's medals.

I stood shivering in my nightie as the wind blew through the broken window. I clasped the empty battered box, turning it over in my hands. Poppy barked an angry tirade at the retreating figures and I felt Bill's loss once more.

Bill always used to say, 'A dog's loyalty will never falter.' I feel the watery June sun warming my arms. Poppy bounds around me in circles, keen to play. I try to hug her, but she wriggles free, eager to keep moving. She flits after a rabbit, then comes lolloping back, with her tongue hanging out.

We clamber up a hill, relishing the warmth and our freedom to roam. Poppy sniffs the air and I drink in the moment, me with my dog.

I run down the hill with my hair flying out behind me. Poppy jumps against my legs, barking excitedly and with her tail whirring.

We are breathless with happiness as we wind our way back through the edge of the poppy field. And then it happens. Without warning. They are hunting pigeons. The gunshot echoes around the valley. Poppy's eyes widen in horror.

Then she bolts. Futilely I call out. But she can only hear the throbbing fear in her head.

Blindly, recklessly she races through the field. Without a backward glance she slides between the hedgerow, hurtling straight towards the main road.

I scream her name. I bolt after her, stumbling clumsily in her wake.

The traffic noise booms louder, screeching nightmarishly and reverberating around the valley.

'Poppy!' I scream. Yet I know it is too late. 'Poppy!'

I stand at the gate and stare.

In the middle of the bend I see another road kill. Another death that would not be noted. A strangled scream is stuck in my throat.

I creep towards the hunched over, matted fur. A scarlet rosette of blood encircles the body.

Another rabbit. So where is Poppy? I look across the road.

There she sits by my car. She looks up with liquid brown eyes that know she has done wrong.

I kneel down and wrap her in my arms. A dog's loyalty will never falter.

For Sue, a great friend and dog lover.

About the author

Linda Flynn has had two humorous novels published: *Hate at First Bite* for 7-9 year-olds, and *My Dad's a Drag* for teenagers. Both won Best First Chapter in The Writers' Billboard competition.

She has six educational books with the Heinemann Fiction Project. In addition she has written for a number of newspapers and magazines, including theatre reviews and several articles on dogs.

Her short stories with Bridge House include: five adult stories: *To Take Flight,* in the *Going Places* anthology, *I knew it in the Bath*, in *Something Hidden*, *Snowdrop* in the anthology *Snowflakes*, *All That Glitters...* in the *Baubles* collection, *The Litter in Glitter* in the Christmas 17 anthology *Gliterary Tales*, as well as *The Wild Ones* for teenagers, in *Devils, Demons and Werewolves*. Two children's short stories: *The Secret Messenger* and *Timid Tim* were included in *Hippo-Dee-Doo-Dah*.

Linda's website is: www.lindaflynn.com

Cider and Chalk

James Phillips

A glass of apple juice

It is hot walking up the hill, even in the shade.
    The still air is thick with the scent of wild garlic.
    We came here as kids.
    'Stay away from the chalk pit!'
    Your mum.
    Easy.
    The top is surrounded by gorse.
    A barrier or a deterrent.
    You emerge from trees into the sun.
    Under your backpack, sweat runs.
    You pass incurious sheep and over the style.
    Once you wouldn't have touched the sides.
    Not anymore.
    You smile; open a bottle.
    The gorse is long gone; there is a fence.
    A barrier and a deterrent.
    Cider arcs and falls.

About the author
James P M Phillips is a writer, musician and live music promoter from North Wales. He blogs about all three of these activities at
https://jamespmphillips.wordpress.com

A Wishing Well

Dawn Knox

Water

The distant hills become one with the night, but at dawn, they emerge from the darkness, silhouetted against the watery light.

I rise, take my water carrier and trek to the well.

One hour later, I am home with my precious cargo.

I set off again.

Three more trips are needed before my family has sufficient water for one day.

Four hours after rising, I set off for school where I will be scolded for tardiness.

I hear that strangers plan to dig a well in my village.

On my walk each morning, I selfishly pray for such a well.

About the author

Dawn's second book *The Great War, 100 stories of 100 words honouring those who lived and died 100 years ago* was published in 2016. She enjoys a writing challenge and has had stories published in various anthologies, including horror and speculative fiction, as well as romances in several women's magazines. Dawn has written a script for a play to commemorate World War One, which has been performed in her home town in Essex, as well as in Germany and France. Married with one son, she lives in Essex.

Play Fair

Stuart Page

Tomato Juice

Board game night. Five sit around a table with a stack of games on. First up: Cooperation in the Desert. 'We won, no thanks to you.'

'You what?'

Next comes Team Tower. 'You're gonna topple it, you're gonna—'

It falls. 'You distracted me!'

After this, Moving in Circles Forever: Extended Edition. 'Money, money, money,' the winner is singing. Someone flips the board and little pieces fly everywhere. The house dog eats a tiny metal car, gets a stomach ache.

'Never again,' one person says.

'See you again next week,' the others say.

About the Author
Stuart Page is an English and Creative Writing graduate from Salford University, currently living near Leeds. He has to write a piece of flash fiction every morning before 9am. If he doesn't, his partner won't let him play Pokémon.

Push
Jasmin L Jackson

Babyccino

'Push!' Paul shouted at his wife, 'You can do this!'

Karen sat on the floor, back braced against the wall, pushing with all her might. Her face was flushed, her teeth gritted. She gave a violent shake of the head.

'I can't, Paul, I just can't,' she gasped, sweat beaded upon her brow, 'I… I don't have the energy to push anymore.'

'One more push, Karen! One more push! I swear that's all it'll take!'

She threw back her head and let out an almighty roar. She was a tiger and she was gonna earn her stripes today. He was right. One more push and it would be over. She could do this. She gave one final push and cried out as her husband released her foot. It was over. It was finally over.

Her foot was in the goddamn shoe.

'And that, Karen,' Paul sighed, trying to catch his breath, 'is why you don't order shoes online.'

About the Author
Jasmin L Jackson is a tea enthusiast who hails from the east of England. She spends her free time writing in coffee shops and swooning over fictional men.

Milk Snatcher

Lisa Williams

Milk served warm

An escaped cow meant we weren't allowed to play outside. Looking back there were a thousand reasons I should have kept quiet but it was a hot day and too much energy trapped inside on such a morning had manifested itself in mischief.

The bottles were warm, glass sweated condensation. The comfortingly unpleasant smell of milk-fat hung over us. We sat, pierced our silver foiled lids. Drank deeply. And then, I raised my hand.

'She took my milk, Miss.'

'Roberts! Come here.'

Margaret got a real roasting that day and although she was innocent, she never did lose that nickname.

About the Author
Lisa Williams. Domestic slattern. Obsessive reader. Writes a bit.

www.noodlebubble.co.uk

Chalk

Alun Williams

Milk

The phrase appeared all over the city, chalked on walls, on sidewalks, and even on the Brooklyn Bridge in letter nine feet high.

'I still love you.'

After a couple of weeks, the media got wind of this and as it was a slow week for news, they aired it.

I recall the pretty CBS blonde anchor-woman pleading with the guy who wrote it to come forward. Perhaps she thought she'd be onto a Pulitzer? Anyhow, even her soulful pleading didn't work. No one came forward.

Every day since a newly chalked phrase was spotted and broadcast.

The world's media sent their camera crews to New York. The chalked phrases became more elaborate. One summer's afternoon, a plane drew the phrase in red smoke over the Statue of Liberty. The country went nuts. New York was now the city of romance. The French were really pissed off with that.

One phrase chalked on the Empire State Building made the cover of *Newsweek* and the *NY Times* offered a reward to whoever could name either the writer or the girl it was intended for. This prompted a response from the gay community who felt maybe they should get in on a piece of the action and handwriting experts were drafted in to argue over whether the writer was male, female and whether or not he/she was gay/straight. Then the black lobby got onto it and the Puerto Ricans, everyone wanted to be the chalker. Damn, the guy was a genius! Bob Dylan wrote a song about it. Best thing he'd written in years. The consensus of opinion was that the writer was male, white and heterosexual, although I never could understand how the so-called experts could work that out from the way the letters were leaning.

Rumours abounded that the writer was a teacher. It was based on the fact that they have access to chalk, but teachers aren't that clever.

What really bugged people, was how the guy could get away with it for so long without being seen. New York is full of cameras. It's like living in an Orwellian state. The only glimpse we got of the guy was a fuzzy, seventeen second black and white film taken from an all-night drugstore camera as he chalked the phrase over the door of a government building. It wasn't clear enough to identify anyone.

Then as quickly as it had started, the writings stopped. People wondered what happened. The media pontificated for a few days then turned to another story. Nothing was heard of this again until three weeks later when another message was chalked up on Trump Towers in six foot high letters.

'I don't love you any more.'

After that there was nothing. People cried openly on the streets. Romance died and the divorce rate soared. Debates were aired on how America wasn't macho any more. Charlton Heston really is a jerk. He thought the mystery chalk writer was undermining our society. Hell yeah, I thought so myself. As if we weren't there already.

Hollywood got in on the act and made a film of course, but it quickly went to video. David Duchovny wasn't right as the MC. He wasn't angry enough. And it had a happy ending and true life isn't Hollywood.

I wish I'd been that guy though. I still love you man.

About the author
Alun Williams Writer of short flash. Published a few times, here and there. Member of critters-bar.com. Lives in North Wales.

In Deep

Michael Hennessy

Still water

Peter was in deep. Very deep.

He had dipped his toe into the murky waters of gambling. Now he was way in over his head. The more he chased his losses, the more he lost... his job, wife, house and his self-respect.

Driving away from the bookie's one night with his usual heavy heart and light wallet, he saw his way out.

The river loomed. The car soared. The black water parted.

As the ringing filled his ears and water filled his lungs, Peter smiled.

No more crippling debt. No more tears of anguish. Now, everything was gone... including his oxygen.

About the author
Michael had a successful career as an award-winning, advertising copywriter. Now he spends his time writing short stories, novels for adults and children, scripts for stage and TV, screenplays and the occasional poem. He is widely travelled and his article about beach dogs in Thailand won The Telegraph Travel 'Just Back' competition. He has been shortlisted, winner and runner-up in many writing competitions and is currently looking for an agent/publisher/producer. His website is currently under construction.

Ruby's Luck

Vicky Jacobson

Bloody Mary

Winner of Canvey Writers first in-house Short Story Competition, 2016.

Editor's Note: This story was chosen as the winner by a group of writers on Canvey Island who voted on a selection of short stories inspired by the theme: The Gift. We had all kinds of stories using the theme in many different ways, but this was chosen because of its unusual theme and one that whetted a few appetites. Part of the prize was publication on this site. So do enjoy...

~~~~~

Ruby picked herself up from the gutter where she'd landed and scowled as the battered old doors of the pub swung shut behind her. She'd been caught trying to dip a customer and the landlord had thrown her out. Not that he had anything against a spot of pickpocketing; he was happy enough to take a cut of what she lifted when she worked his premises, but she'd committed the sin of getting caught.

'I can't be seen to condone robbing the customers, girl – it's bad for business,' he'd said as he'd manhandled her towards the door.

Cold rain was falling from the sky now, lashing the cobblestones and running through the filthy gutter as Ruby straightened and wiped her muddy hands on her dress. She had to get out of the rain.

She turned towards The Ten Bells further down the street where, hopefully, trade might be a bit better. Barely into November and already the temperature was falling fast; at this rate, there'd be snow on the ground before Christmas. Ruby shivered in the night air and pulled her shawl tighter round her shoulders.

Pushing open the door to The Bells, Ruby entered the smoky room, grateful for the warmth from the hearth. She looked around to see whether there were any likely punters about and, seeing a face she recognised, made her way across the room towards him.

'Hi, handsome,' she said, 'wanna buy a girl a drink.'

'Sorry, sweetheart, I'm flat broke – no chink at all,' he replied, shaking his pockets.

'Not even enough for a tuppenny upright, darling.'

Ruby leaned in close to whisper these words, she had to be careful, the landlord had warned her before about soliciting and she knew he'd throw her out into the cold, rainy night if he caught her.

'Sorry,' shrugged the man and turned back to his beer.

Ruby moved away, scanning the crowded room for fresh meat. She spotted a man in a long, dark astrakhan coat on the other side of the room and, even from this distance, she could see he was dressed well. She turned and started to head in his direction but was pulled up short as the landlord caught her by the arm.

'Ere, if you're touting for trade, out you go.'

'I've just come in to get warm and get out of the rain, John,' she replied, pulling her arm free but when she looked back towards the toff in the corner, she saw he'd disappeared and swore softly.

Later that night, Ruby was still walking the streets. In the past, she'd always seemed to have a gift for attracting good luck – which she thought, maybe, was to make up for her beginnings. A foundling, she'd been brought up in an orphanage and put to work at the age of seven. There was never enough to eat and the regular beatings had left her with a scar to one side of her face and a slight limp. Hardly surprising then that she'd taken off as soon as she was old enough. She knew she wasn't unique; there must have been thousands of kids like her – but, as she'd grown older, she'd begun to notice that, somehow, things always seemed to go in her favour. Life had never been easy but whenever it started to get really desperate, something always turned up. She thought back to the time when, unwell and unable to work, she'd found half-a-crown lying on the pavement – just as her money had run out. The gin hadn't stopped flowing that night and Ruby chuckled at the memory and thanked her guardian angel for working so hard. Of course, the unexpected windfall didn't last long, but there'd always – so far at least – been a next time.

The rain was falling steadily now but Ruby's luck had yet to put in an appearance. She'd been in one pub after another and had walked the streets in between for hours but had found no takers.

Finally though, weaving along Commercial Street, she saw, up ahead, the well-dressed man who had been in The Bells earlier and thought perhaps her luck was kicking in at last. He was standing on the corner outside The Brit and now wore a soft felt hat pulled down over his eyes. She felt a quick flash of hope that, maybe, standing there was her night's rent and she picked up her pace. Before she could reach him, though, Mary from Miller's Court rounded the corner of Dorset Street and they'd started chatting.

Mary was young and good-looking with fair hair; always neatly dressed, tonight, she'd cheered up this dreary winter's eve with a brightly coloured shawl. Given a choice between the two of them, Ruby knew who she'd have chosen if she were the cove.

She saw him put a hand on Mary's shoulder; they laughed and then turned to walk down the street together. Watching her night's lodging disappear with another judy, Ruby pressed her lips together as a stab of anger shot through her. She knew that Mary, at least, had a room of her own and wouldn't need to come out again tonight whereas without doss money Ruby, herself, had nowhere to go.

The rain was falling heavily now and Ruby needed to find shelter. It was past two in the morning and she knew there wasn't much chance of picking up any business now, especially with the weather the way it was. She held out her hand and watched the cold, grey rain bounce off it. The few farthings she'd had in her pocket had been enough for a couple of drinks and the cheap booze would help to keep her warm as she resigned herself to sleeping out. She headed for a covered passageway she'd had to use occasionally before. She sighed, and wrapping herself up as best she could, settled down for the night in the entrance to one of the many courtyards in the rookery, where at least it was dry.

Tonight, her luck seemed to have deserted her entirely and Ruby was afraid that she might have lost her gift for good.

She slipped into an uneasy, dreamless sleep. Somewhere around four o'clock, she was roused from her slumber by the sound of a woman in distress calling out from somewhere close by. That wasn't unusual for Dorset Street though and as it quickly fell silent again, she soon drifted back to sleep. She slept on, fitfully, for another couple of hours, until the night cops found her and moved her on.

Ten days later, Ruby joined the vast throng outside St Leonard's Church in Shoreditch for the funeral of Mary Jane Kelly – latest victim of The Ripper.

People – even those who couldn't possibly have known her – were openly weeping and men stood clutcheing their hats as the coffin appeared. The whole city had been shocked by the reports of Mary's death and thousands had turned out to pay their respects to this poor young woman who had met such a tragic end.

Ruby was there, not only because she'd known, and liked, Mary but also because she knew that if Mary hadn't rounded the corner when she did, the body now lying in that coffin would have been hers.

Clutching a posy of wild flowers picked from the churchyard, she followed the funeral cortege, along with what appeared to be the rest of the East End. They were headed for St Patrick's Catholic Cemetery on the outskirts of the city, in Leytonstone, where Mary Kelly would be laid to rest.

She stood back from the graveside in the chill afternoon air for a very long time until all the other mourners had left and the grave had been filled in. Finally, when she was completely alone, she stepped forward and placed her small bundle of flowers on the fresh mound of earth marking the grave.

'God bless Mary, rest in peace and thank you,' she whispered.

Ruby was happy that she still had her gift and that it had been protecting her all along. She would always be sorry that, this time, the price of her good fortune had been someone else's life but she was grateful for the second chance and determined not to waste it, if only for Mary's sake.

The man in the astrakhan coat had been in the paper after the killing and Ruby thought she probably knew who the Ripper was. Speaking out definitely wasn't a risk she could afford to take, though – not only was it very doubtful she would be believed, it was also extremely likely to get her killed.

Ruby needed to leave Whitechapel. That much was clear. Following the hearse through London, she'd seen the slums, with the dirty hovels and dingy alleys, fall away behind as the streets ahead improved mile by mile.

She knew nothing about Leytonstone but Ruby was an enterprising girl and, eyeing up her surroundings, quickly decided that it would do. Besides, she thought, with a shrewd smile, something was bound to turn up – it usually did.

About the author
Vicky is a retired legal secretary with two grown-up children. She has always had a desire to write but only really got started when she joined Canvey Writers earlier this year. This story was chosen by the group as the WINNER of their first in-house writing competition in 2016. Vicky's previous story published on this site, *Dialling 999*, was selected for *The Best of CaféLit 5* and was her first publication.

Elvis's son

Z.L. Porter

Pepsi Cola

It was Saturday night. I had been working my residency slot at the Rio in Streatham. My act went backwards through the three eras of Elvis, starting with the 1970s, then the 1960s, and then the 1950s. The crowd loved me. Take it from me, my *Viva Las Vegas* is unsurpassed by any Elvis Tribute Artist you will ever see, anywhere.

When I went into *Love Me Tender* I saw desire flash through some of the women's eyes, saw it in the way their bodies stiffened with surprise and then relaxed. It disconcerted them of course, it always does, but there was lust in the air, moist and fragrant. A hen party was grouped around a table, all tinsel and feathers and headbands with floppy cocks on them. Some of those girls were giggling, some were open-mouthed, and some of them kind of shape-shifted into tender, furry animals before my eyes. When I came off stage (one encore, two standing ovations), I was pretty sure I was going to get lucky.

I swept back to my dressing room. My plan was to change into my bespoke 1968 Comeback Special black leather outfit and wait it out for ten minutes before I returned to mingle with the bride-to-be and her friends.

But he was there, waiting for me: my nemesis. He

was sitting in my faux-leather swivel chair, eyes trained like snipers on the mirror waiting for me to come in.

'How did you get in here?'

'Walked straight in.'

'Why?'

'Come to pick a bone.'

I did not answer. I pulled a hard-backed chair from the corner of the room, deliberately slowly so that the wooden legs scraped against the floorboards. I wheeled him back a couple of paces and sat before the mirror. I did not want to take off my make-up and sideburns – they were critical to my chat up routine – so I just lined up the acetone and baby wipes on the counter and waited for him to begin.

'There's only one Dwarf Elvis in London and that's me,' he said.

'Let me guess. Business is bad. You've got no bookings. And you're blaming me.'

'It's your bloody fault!'

'It's not my fault, Anthony.' I pronounced the 'th' of his name just as he liked it. 'It's not my fault that you can't sing.'

'I can sing!'

'Not like me. Not like the King.'

'It boils down to this. When people book a Dwarf Elvis Tribute Artist, they book you. You're everywhere. Residency here at the Rio. Monthly slot at the Clapham Grand. Top of the Google search. And you're not even a dwarf! You're taking my work.'

I had a feeling it would come down to this, that I am not, technically, a dwarf. 4'10 is a dwarf in my book, but I am perfectly proportioned (everywhere, baby), and I do not have a genetic condition, so the correct term for me in current medical vogue is 'very small person' or 'little person'. It used to be 'midget' but apparently that's offensive.

'I get booked, Anthony, because I am classy,' I replied. 'I am an artist in a small package. I am one of the chosen ones.'

'I am going to sue you for misrepresentation.'

I did not flinch. I decided to humour him. 'You've done your research.'

'Yes, I have.'

'You know, you should talk to my agent. We discussed it when he signed me. He thinks that 'Dwarf Elvis' rolls off the tongue better than any of the alternatives.' I picked up a can of Elnett and sprayed it into my quiff.

'But it's not what you are. You're lying to people.'

'Oh please. You're lying to people when you tell them you can sing! Anyway, if I change my stage name and you suddenly become the only Dwarf Elvis in town, people will book you thinking it's me, which sounds to me like misrepresentation.'

'They won't care.'

'Until you open your bloody mouth! And then maybe I'll sue you for ruining my reputation. Here's an idea. Why don't you call yourself Prick Elvis?'

'Don't push me, Simon.' He slid off the swivel chair and started walking towards me.

'Or Cocksucker Elvis?'

He punched me. It stung a bit but I could take it. I grabbed him by the throat. I lift weights for an hour a day. It wasn't hard to push him down onto the floor and straddle his chest.

'Now get this straight,' I said to him, holding his jaw in one hand, 'I am Dwarf Elvis. You can sue if you want to. But I can bloody well sing like the King. I heard his voice, Anthony, his ac-tu-al voice, telling me that I was one of his chosen sons. And he was right. Because did you hear those standing ovations back then? Do you appreciate what you're up against here? You don't stand a cat's chance in hell. Now, why don't you fuck off home and we'll pretend this never happened?'

He scampered away after that, mumbling something about my not hearing the last of it. I'm not worried.

I know what you're thinking. You're right. He had a point and I showed him no mercy. There are winners and there are losers in this world. And you want me to apologise for being a winner?

About the Author
Z. L. Porter lives in North Yorkshire with her husband, children, and chickens.

That Friday Night

Roger Noons

Just plain orange juice

A unique cabaret, just after ten o'clock on that warm summer's night. All the street came out and the pubs emptied early after a Midland Red bus became wedged beneath the railway bridge, just yards from Cradley Station.

'Novice driver, mustn't know the route.'

'Careered past my window.'

'Is anybody hurt?'

'The driver's run away.'

Sergeant Bills rubbed all his chins, wondering what to do.

Behind No. 20 Cokeland Place, William Clift, no bus driver, but a chain maker by trade, didn't even have a licence, was counting out ten shilling notes.

He enjoyed a wager did Uncle Bill.

About the Author
Roger Noons is a regular contributor to CaféLit, wowing us with many 100 worders and some longer ones – and you can also read his stories in our *Best of CaféLit* series.

Pumpkin Soup with a Dash of Magic

Helen Laycock

Pumpkin soup

Shelley hated basement living.

By five, the light had faded. She stood at the window and craned up to street level. Lit pumpkins swung next to little feet while she was cooped in her musty flat browsing lonely hearts ads and stirring soup.

The gloom seemed to drop heavily and squat on the cobbles. A clump of moss needed clearing from the damp steps. She slipped out, hugging her cardigan closed.

A toad!

Shelley squealed.

No sooner had she run inside and slammed the door than there was a knock.

'Harry Prince,' said the handsome stranger. 'Just moved in upstairs.'

About the author
A regular contributor to CaféLit, Helen Laycock writes for both adults and children. She has published three short story collections as well as several mystery/adventure books for readers of 8-12. She has had work published in a further ten anthologies, as well as online, and has had success in writing competitions with poetry, flash, short stories and plays.

Predictive Text

Gill James

A pot of builder's tea

'Good. That will do for today, I think. Shall we make another appointment?' Sandy opened the calendar on her phone.

Mrs Adams had been pottering about in the kitchen. The door was open into the dining area. She took her cue.

'What do you think, then Jon? One more before the holiday?'

Jon nodded.

Mrs Adams turned to Sandy. 'Is that all right with you?'

'What about Friday 22nd? Same time?'

Mrs Adams and Jon both nodded.

'Good. That's a date then.' Sandy started typing. The predictive text did the usual trick. No matter. She was used to it. She knew what it meant. She couldn't be bothered to change it.

Two days later Sandy's phone rang. *There must be a problem with Jon's lesson,* she thought as the name of the caller appeared on her phone. 'Hello, Mrs Beans, how can I help you?'

Sandy blushed as a flustered Mrs Adams muttered something about a wrong number.

And to think that it was Jon who had told her that the latest word for 'cool' was 'book'.

About the author

Gill James writes for adults, children and young adults. She has recently retired as a senior lecturer at the University of Salford. She edits for Bridge House, The Red Telephone and CaféLit. Follow her blog:
www.gilljameswriter.eu

An Alternative Halloween

Janet Bunce

Witches' brew!

We gathered together for the 31st October.

No-one knew specifically why we did it.

Someone who had dusted off an old book said it was about the Day of the Dead.

But for us it was the time of life.

We had spent weeks, months, years in a catacomb- no-one actually knew.

This day we could stretch our arms, legs and faces.

We could walk on earth and reconnect with the world.

Sometimes scarily we heard the screams of the living.

We assumed they were harming each other but occasionally we realised from their faces we were wrong!

About the author
Janet has had several short stories published by CaféLit and very much enjoys writing. She particularly enjoys writing in the horror/sci-fi genre.

Treasure Hunt

Alyson Faye

Dark Mozart

Our little gang of scavengers always take a vote before we head out. We're democratic that way.

That January day, the waste ground behind the newly built skyscraper won. It was Billy who found the doll, lying in the frosty tipped grass. Weak sunshine gleamed on her glassy eyes.

Shoving it at me, Billy rubbed his hands on his denims, 'Yuk, it's slimy. Here Jem. You have it.'

None of us had toys, so this was real treasure. Grabbing the doll's tiny hand, I instantly recognized it. From the many 'Missing' posters pinned up. The lost girl was cuddling it.

About the author
Alyson writes mainly flash fiction and short stories. Her work has appeared on *Tubeflash* online*, on the premises*, *Three Drops journa*l; Raging Aardvark's new anthology *Twisted Tales* and *Alfie Dog*. Some of her stories are available as podcasts.

Recognition

Gill James

A glass of red wine

She stuck the fat hardback under her arm and picked up the free newspaper. She'd only bought the book three days before as an airport special and it would be callous to have read it before it officially came out at home. Plus she didn't want to finish it. It was too good. She didn't want to lose its interesting characters and its colourful setting.

The flight was to be twenty minutes late, they said.

The man sitting opposite looked harassed. He was writing in a notebook.

Must be a writer as well, she thought. Should she approach him? Initiate a chat? Swap notes?

Mmm. Maybe not. He glowered at her as she attempted a smile. And he was very twitchy.

Oh come on. The plane was only twenty minutes late. Maybe he was a nervous flyer?

Soon she was engrossed in an article about the new economy and was surprised when they were asked to board the plane.

Settled in her seat and now a little nervous herself about take-off she decided to turn back to her book. She'd used the rear flap to mark her place. She opened the book, then oh my god, she recognised the face in the author biography. The man with the note-book.

She wondered whether she might find him after take-off and ask for his autograph.

About the author
Gill James writes for adults, children and young adults. She has recently retired as a senior lecturer at the University of Salford. She edits for Bridge House, The Red Telephone and CaféLit. Follow her blog:
www.gilljameswriter.eu

Walk a Mile

Patsy Collins

A big mug of wishful thinking

Walk a mile in someone's shoes before you truly know them. That's what 'they' say. Maybe they're right; I wouldn't know.

I'd like to wear ballet pumps. Stand on the points of my toes, even if it gave me calluses. Or don flippers to swim in warm pools, or cold, dangerous seas. Skis sound fun, rushing downhill so fast my eyes wouldn't focus on the whitescape flashing by. Maybe I'd break my leg. I wouldn't mind the cast, not if it came after trying the skis. I'd put on trainers and run, Army boots and march, or struggle upstream in waders if I could.

Look at my shoes. Pretty, lots of colours. If you want to know me, put them on. Don't walk a mile. Or even a step. I can't you see. To know me, sit in my shoes and think where you'll walk when you've taken them off.

About the author
Patsy is a novelist, short story writer and co-author of *From Story Idea to Reader – an accessible guide to writing fiction.* http://getBook.at/FSITR

Resolutions

Roger Noons

A glass of champagne

'Made any New Year resolutions, Phil?'

'Yeah, quite a few.'

'Such as?'

'I'm going to treat everyone in the pub when I go to the New Inn on a Friday night.'

'Right, I'll be there,' Alan grinned.

'I'm going to help the missus with housework and ironing.'

'Wow!'

'And I'll give her more housekeeping money, take her to the supermarket every week.'

'Bloody hell mate, this is beginning to sound serious.'

Phil beamed, took another swallow of his lager.

'And are you going to stop telling lies?'

'Ah, now I don't know if I can go that far.'

About the Author
Roger Noons is a regular contributor to CaféLit, wowing us with many 100 worders and some longer ones – and you can also read his stories in our *Best of CaféLit* series.

All Things Wise and Wonderful
Gill James

Americano

'Uncle Gary, he bit you,' screeched Rosie. 'He's a mean old thing. After you agreed to look after him for Benji.'

She's being hysterical again, thought Toby. Even so, his heart was beating fast as well. Would that wild thing that called itself a dog attack him next?

'Oh, he didn't mean anything by it, did you, Scruff?' said Uncle Gary. 'He'd had a funny old life, until Benji took him in, didn't you old chap?' Uncle Gary tickled the ears of the rough-haired dog. Scruff's tail shot down between his legs, and then he started wagging it tentatively. Uncle Garry patted him once more and then pulled his hand back and sucked it. He waved the hand in the air. 'Look, hardly drawn blood,' he said grinning. 'Better keep the cats away from him, though.'

On cue, the cat flap went. There was the familiar sound of a high-speed Flix, followed by a frantic mewing.

'Oh no!' cried Rosie.

Toby followed her into the hallway. That sound meant only one thing: she had caught something - probably a mouse.

Uncle Gary quickly directed Scruff to the lounge.

'Stay!' he bellowed.

It wasn't a mouse. It was a bird. It sat on the hall carpet, blinking. Its feathers were all puffed up and it seemed to be taking deep breaths. Flix pawed at it, then started to circle it.

Rosie was cowering behind Uncle Gary. She hated it when there was a bird loose in the house. She hated the way the wings fluttered. Several times Toby had had to chase one out.

'It's a baby,' said Uncle Gary. 'A young robin.'

Uncle Gary bent down to pick the bird up. It fluttered up into the air.

'Open the door quickly,' said Uncle Gary.

Toby rushed to the door and opened it. The outside air seemed to push the little bird back in, though. Uncle Gary grabbed the newspaper, which was sticking through the letterbox and waved the bird towards the open door. It managed to flutter a little and then landed on the drive.

'It'll probably recover and fly back to its parents soon,' said Uncle Gary. 'Give that cat a ball of paper to play with to keep her mind off it.'

Toby took a piece of paper out of the recycling bin. He screwed it up and threw it at the cat. Soon, she was chasing it all over the place.

Toby went back up to his room. He had some homework to do. But from his room, he could easily see on to the drive. He found it difficult to concentrate and kept looking down to see whether the bird had moved. At last, it seemed to flutter its wings a little.

Toby settled down to his history project. He heard Rosie go out with Uncle Gary and Scruff, and he could hear his mother pottering about in the kitchen making the sausage rolls and quiches for grandma's seventieth birthday party. It would be best if he could get this history project finished first. But it was boring, oh so boring, and soon he fell asleep.

It was Flix and Sheeba having a pop at each other that woke him. They didn't do that these days so much as they used to. They were both adopted cats, and after a lot of snarling and growling, when they were first introduced to each other, they had learned to ignore each other most of the time. Sheeba was doing her usual trick of sitting on her hind legs and boxing. Flix was fighting like a trooper.

'Don't you realise she's twice as big as you, you daft cat,' he said to Flix, picking her up and carrying her to the lounge. It was then that he saw what had probably caused the tension. He was there again, in the middle of the hall carpet, looking even more disturbed this time, but once again blinking quietly and breathing deeply. Toby could see that part of his wing was torn.

'You poor thing,' he said. He opened the kitchen door to let Sheeba in

'I don't want any cats in here, thank you,' shouted Mum. 'It's unhygienic when I'm baking.'

'They've brought something in,' Toby shouted back.

'Well get rid of it,' shouted Mum.

'What do you think I'm trying to do?' Toby muttered, slamming the door. But what to do next?

He wasn't as silly as Rosie about birds flying about in the house. But he didn't think he could pick it up with his bare hands like Uncle Gary had tried to. It would feel funny if it tried to fly away - or worse still, did a poo on him.

'What is it?' he heard Mum shout. 'Get rid of it quickly. I want this cat out of here.'

She opened the door and Sheeba darted out.

'Mum!' shouted Toby. His mother grabbed Sheeba, depositing flour all over her black fur.

'This is a nuisance while I'm trying to make sausage rolls!' Mum shouted.

He would have to do something.

'Clear it out! Clear it out!' Mum almost screeched now. She was talking as if the poor thing was a piece of rubbish. But at least that gave him an idea. He opened the door to the cupboard under the stairs and took out the dustpan and brush. Carefully, he pushed the bird on to the pan with the brush.

'It's all right. It's all right,' he whispered to the bird.

It sat quietly on the dustpan, not moving.

'Put it as high up on the tree as you can,' called his mother as he opened the door.

Toby chose the fig tree, which hung over the drive from next door. It was quite a job getting the little fellow to perch on the branch. But he did at last.

When Toby got back inside the two cats were curled up asleep in the lounge, Sheeba in front of the fire, Flix perched precariously on the back of the sofa.

Crisis over! He had better get back to that history project. Soon, he was back in the world of the Romans, marvelling at how their heating systems worked. He was just finishing the last sentence when he heard Uncle Gary's key on the lock.

'Toby!' his uncle called upstairs.

Toby rushed downstairs. Uncle Gary was still in the porch. He was using an old towel to rub down one very muddy Scruff.

'Seen any more of that young bird?' he asked. 'Only its parents are outside, chuntering about something.'

Toby explained what had happened.

'Yeah, well, the trouble is,' said Uncle Gary, 'Robins always nest near the ground. Poor little blighter would probably try to get back home - and he'd risk getting killed on the way. He obviously hasn't made it yet. That's why those two are kicking up such a row.'

'Should we keep Flix and Sheeba in?' asked Toby.

'Not a good idea,' said Uncle Gary. 'That would be cruel to them. They're used to being able to go in and out. Anyway, they need to be able to get away from old Scruff.'

There was not really anything they could do.

Toby soon forgot about the bird. There was a good film on the television. He didn't think about it again, until just after tea. He was helping to clear the tea things off when he heard a frantic squawking outside. He looked through the patio doors. Flix was there with the bird between her paws. He thought it must be dead. She was batting it, like she did with a paper ball, to make it move so that she could chase it.

The two robins were circling round her, clearly angry.

How can such little things make so much noise? thought Toby. The birds were now screeching really loudly. *Crikey,* he thought, *they're going to peck her eyes out.* Quickly, he picked the cat up. The birds immediately shut up. They were staring at him. *Perhaps they're going to have a go at me now,* he thought. *Better get out of here.* He started to walk back towards the house, holding tightly to Flix who was now the one who was protesting.

Just as he was about to open the patio door, the little bird moved. It hopped uncertainly. The bigger birds moved towards it. Their child was still alive, but they wouldn't be able to carry it back to the nest.

Toby dropped the cat just inside the door and shut it quickly.

'Okay, you guys,' he said. 'Show me where to take

him and I'll put him there.' The male robin puffed up his red breast, making himself look important. The smaller bird just sat and blinked at him.

Toby bent down to the baby bird.

'Come on, little fella,' he said. This time it didn't bother him picking up the little bird. He was surprised at how soft and cuddly it actually felt. It was taking very deep breaths again. Toby thought he could feel its heart beating. It didn't move at all as Toby looked round for the tree which might hold his nest.

The two parents followed Toby, circling round him, looking at him suspiciously, but not making any noise. The red-breasted bird suddenly landed on a branch of the old crab-apple tree.

'Is this it, then?' asked Toby. He could see a mound of leaves. He gently laid the bird down in the bed. 'There you go then.' The bird blinked at him. *He's such a brave little fighter,* thought Toby. He winced to himself as he saw the blood on the bird's wing.

The smaller adult bird hopped down next to the nest.

Toby went back into the house. He didn't have to decide whether to keep Flix and Sheeba in. It had just started to rain and both cats and Scruff decided that it was best to sleep away the time.

There were no more dramas that day.

'Well, those birds seem to have kept quiet this evening,' said Uncle Gary after it had got dark. 'I wonder if the little fella survived?' He was putting some more antiseptic on the place where Scruff had bit him.

'Shouldn't you go and see the doctor about that?' asked Mum.

'Naw!' said Uncle Gary. 'He's hardly grazed the skin. He stopped when he realised what he was doing. He didn't mean it personally.'

'Hmm. Biting the hand that feeds him,' said Mum.

'No!' retorted Uncle Gary. 'Just being himself. A poor animal who'd been let down by human beings. Then he remembered that, actually, we're okay.'

'You're amazing, Uncle Gary,' said Rosie, rushing over and giving her uncle a hug.

'Steady on,' said Uncle Gary, almost spilling the antiseptic.

But she was right. Uncle Gary was amazing.

The next morning, Toby woke up as Sheeba pounded on his door. She was mewing loudly and Toby could swear he heard her say 'Let me in! Let me in!' Then he heard Flix making a fuss downstairs, followed by an 'Oh no!' from Rosie.

Rubbing his eyes, Toby made his way down to see what all the fuss was about. Why were people making so much noise at this time of the morning? He glanced at the clock. It was only half past six.

Uncle Gary was standing there in his dressing gown.

'What a shame,' he said. 'So he didn't make it after all.'

Toby felt slightly sick as he looked at the body of the little bird. It lay stiffly on the hall carpet.

'You wicked thing, Flix,' said Uncle Gary. He tickled the little cat's ears. She started purring and rubbed her cheek against Uncle Gary's leg.

Toby was wide-awake now. It was just so unfair. It would have been much better if Flix had killed him first time. Instead, the poor animal had had all that fear and pain. That would have been okay if he had survived. To die after all of that didn't seem worth the bother.

Rosie was howling by now. She stamped her foot at Flix.

'Go away, you nasty cruel cat,' she shouted.

Flix looked startled for a moment, and then ambled off with her nose in the air towards her food bowl.

'Well, I don't know about you,' said Uncle Gary. 'But I could do with a cup of tea. Care to join me?'

Toby nodded. He didn't dare say anything. There was a great danger that he was going to cry. It was all very well - Rosie making such a fuss. But it would just look so absolutely silly on a big lad like him who was about to go up to the comprehensive school next year. Especially in front of Uncle Gary.

He watched as his uncle put the kettle on, and then brushed the corpse of the little bird into the dustpan. He took a Tesco's bag out of the cupboard and dropped the dead bird into it and then went out to the bin with it.

No funeral service for you, then, thought Toby.

Uncle Gary finished making the tea and he poured out an orange juice for Rosie.

'Come on,' he said to Rosie. 'It's just nature, you know. Let's see if we can find you a funny cartoon to take your mind off it.'

Toby and Uncle Gary sat and watched the cartoon with Rosie as they drank their tea and she drank her orange juice. She had forgotten all about the dead bird, or so it seemed. She was watching *Tom and Jerry,* of all things.

When Toby got back up to his room half an hour later, Sheeba was fast asleep on his bed. She stirred as he moved into the room. She stood up, stretched and mewed at him as if saying 'Hello.'

Toby sat down on the bed beside her.

'You lot cause trouble,' he said. She stared at him with her big round eyes. He always thought she looked like an owl. Could she be the child that was born of the Owl and the Pussycat from the poem? 'That poor little bird!'

'Miaow!' said Sheeba. She went up to him and nuzzled his face. Automatically, he stretched his hand out and smoothed her thick, silky fur.

'Miaow!' she said again. Or was it 'I know.'? She licked him on the nose.

Toby sighed. 'I guess you were just being yourself,' he said. 'You were born to hunt' It didn't stop him feeling sad about the bird. But he couldn't feel cross with this beautiful creature. At least now he understood about Uncle Gary and Scruff. And about a few other things as well.

Sheeba butted him under the chin and rubbed her cheek against his.

''Sright,' he heard her say.

About the author
Gill James writes for adults, children and young adults. She has recently retired as a senior lecturer at the University of Salford. She edits for Bridge House, The Red Telephone and CaféLit. Follow her blog:
www.gilljameswriter.eu

Shadow

David Deanshaw

A cup of wine

Dan Briggs heaved a sigh of relief as he reached up to release the heavy metal hooks which held open the large double doors of The Swan. Closing time at last!

The customers, in fact the whole world, seemed to be convinced that the Christmas trade made publicans laugh all the way to the bank. If only they knew! Tonight, Christmas Eve had been hectic. True, takings were high and that should be good for him, his business and his family. Family. That word echoed round in his mind until his head was spinning.

Outwardly he enjoyed his role as the local publican, being at the centre of the village life along with the church. Inwardly his heart was aching. Still he had a public to serve and a position in the community to maintain. He had spent some of his profits to ensure that there was a room for families when necessary. He was also the sponsor of the village darts team. There were a number of small rooms scattered round the old pub, often used by village organisations for their committee meetings; they all added to the takings. Everything one would require in a small village pub. Most of his regulars

71

were local farmers but some were commuters who enjoyed the peace and quiet of the countryside and being away from their busy city lives. His North Country candour meant that he spoke his mind at all times and they appreciated him all the more for that.

He had been delighted with the style that he had brought to the pub. There was now a long bar of polished walnut. The brass beer pumps stood proud and highly polished, each with the name of the sponsoring brewery. Behind the bar there was a high mirror which enabled all the immaculately clean glasses and shorts bottles to shine brightly. Alongside the bar there were a few high stools made of beech. These too were polished and maintained regularly. After all, some of his farmer customers were broad in the beam!

As he stood in the doorway, the light from the porch cut a giant wedge in the snow. With his arms akimbo and feet planted wide apart, his eyes followed his shadow as it stretched out across the snow and rose up the little hill in front of the pub. The sky was a speckled deep blue carpet and the cold night air caused him to breathe deeply. As he exhaled, his breath became a white mist. The security light behind him producing a searchlight effect.

Family!
The ache in his heart weighed heavily as he

recollected how life had changed for him over the last twelve months.

Christmas seemed to engender the notion that families should be together.

This year was going to be different. For the first time since the children had been born, he would be on his own. He honestly believed in the wisdom, perhaps nobility, by which he had gone without to ensure that their future could be more certain.

In his early days in Yorkshire the family had two rooms upstairs and two down with an additional scullery at the rear. It was in this room that he used to see his mother working away at not only the family's washing, but piles of clothes from others in order to make ends meet. There too he had seen his father digging not only his own allotment, but tilling others so he could add to the subsistence life style in rural Yorkshire.

There he had been brought up to accept the old fashioned values of loyalty, respect and the sanctity of the family unit.

Later he had moved south and bought a small village pub with living accommodation over. He and his wife had had such great dreams as they started their family. They both eagerly took part in helping the children with their homework.

Then tragedy struck them with his wife's illness and her desperate fight for life through terrible pain. Eventually the cancer had won and relieved her of all her agony. She had died, leaving him to bring up two children in their early teenage years. He had grieved in private to shelter his children, but the pain was always just under the surface. Especially now, when he felt he had nothing.

Indeed, life had been tough ever since. He had scrimped to provide his children with the best education that he could afford. Most parents expected their teenage children to get part-time jobs, but not Dan.

'I will provide. Just use the time to study, gain real skills and create a better life for yourselves than your mother and I have had!'

That message was hammered home for years as they grew up.

When both Sarah and Peter went to university, Dan was fit to burst with pride. He should have been looking forward to them coming home for Christmas, but he had sent them into an exile he now desperately regretted. He was not a religious man in the normally accepted sense. He was not 'spiritually certain' or anything like that, but he had been brought up to believe that forgiveness was only possible with repentance.

His mind wandered back to that first blow.

Dan's first inkling that trouble was brewing was when Sarah came home unexpectedly from the social services job she had started only a few months earlier. Whilst he missed his daughter being away from him, he knew she had a life of her own to live, so her sudden arrival meant that she was missing him or that she a real problem.

University had been a tough process for a girl leaving home for the first time, especially one whose mother had died when she was very young. But she had survived three years of study and her year out had been spent looking at how local councils provided support and care for people in need. With her degree in hand, she had applied to work in a town some distance away. She stayed in touch with her dad but had grown the wings of independence since she had left home. The director had set her some tough tasks and she was relishing the challenge. These tasks took her to situations she had never experienced before, including locations off the beaten track – gipsy encampments, transport cafés – children in those situations were often neglected or allowed to run wild.

'Oh, Dad, you would not believe some of the jobs I have to do. Some people don't deserve to have children. Some of the places I've visited would make you shudder.' The poverty and deprivation she had seen reminded her of the stories Dad used to tell them about his own childhood. Her boss had thought she might be a bit posh due to the way she spoke, especially bearing in mind the kind of poor and sometime feckless families with whom she would be dealing. However he soon discovered that he was delighted with the insights she brought to her understanding of the problems and, more importantly, the solutions she proposed.

'Darling, please look after yourself. I worry about you. Yet, at the same time, I am so proud of you.'

On that quiet afternoon, almost three months after Sarah had left home full of hopes and self-confidence, Dan was shocked to see her walk through his front door

'Dad, I have something very important to tell you. I've met a nice chap named Fred, who wants to marry me. I met him at a transport café on one of my assignments.'

'So soon? Please at least develop your skills and get some experience under your belt.' Dan was aghast.

'Dad, I'm sorry but I'm pregnant.'

Dan had a sharp intake of breath and could feel a lump the size of a cricket ball in his throat. Dan was close to tears, the slap of his hand on his forehead echoed round the small living area over the bar.

'So all that scrimping was for nothing! How could you?'

'Dad, I am really, really sorry, but I do love him!' Sarah too knew that tears were coming and soon as she watched her father shake his head.

'Dad, it is my life.' She was spluttering now.

Dan looked at her, his ashen face shaking. He lifted his right hand to his face, his thumb in his right eye and his index finger in his left, to wipe the tears. Suddenly, he could find nothing to say. The maelstrom of emotions was tearing him apart inside. There was disappointment – bitter, bitter disappointment, as well as shame. Sarah had been popular in the village, now what would people say? – The shame of it!

'Dad, I do love you, but it's my life.'

'Alright, alright, you've already made that clear!'

'We are just having a quiet ceremony, no fuss.'

She left in tears. As she looked back, her father's face was set like granite. She pondered whether perhaps this was the beginning of a new life for both of them.

The events which followed took both of them by surprise, bringing unhappiness as well as bitterness.

Less than two years after the modest registry office ceremony in front of just two witnesses from the transport café, Fred had found another woman and Sarah, destitute, had returned to her dad.

He turned her away.

Then he called her back.

'If you come back, you'll have to work. This place is too big for me as it is. That child will have to go – let that no-good father bring it up.'

'Dad, do you know just how brutal that sounds?

You know that I'd be grateful for a roof over my head. Look, soon it'll be Christmas. When you see your grandson playing with his toys near the Christmas tree, I'm sure you'll think differently. I just hope you can forgive me. Especially at this time of year. Besides, Peter will be coming home for Christmas and that will help. Peter's presence always makes you happy.'

But Dan was adamant and Sarah again left in tears. Dan too wanted to understand why he had been so harsh on his own flesh and blood. But Sarah had not considered his feelings in the matter, so why should he spare a thought for hers?

Some months later an unexpected letter arrived.

Dear Dad,

I am really sorry that you have decided that you want nothing to do with your grandson Daniel. He is lovely boy with a cheerful manner and he is starting to talk and walk. He has a round face just like yours.

I am living in a social services hostel and being looked after and supported by the very team with which I worked. The Team Leader is very supportive and in some ways they see me and my situation as a good test case to see how well or otherwise the 'system' is working.

Daniel seems to get on with the other babies in the nursery. I spend lots of time with him even though I am working part-time with the team. I have access to a laptop so when he is asleep I am able to earn

something for my keep and ensure that Daniel has a
safe base.
   I really had thought that seeing Daniel crawling
around the Christmas tree would have appealed to you.
   Lots of love,
   Sarah xx

Dan's son Peter was in his final year at agricultural
college. Every time he came home he would tell his
dad how much he wanted to put all his new theories
into practice. During his time at college, he had been
sponsored to travel and work in various countries,
some in Europe as well as Africa.

Dan's Christmas present for his son that year was
a formidable one.

Alex Hughes, one of Dan's regular customers,
owned the farm next door to the pub. Alex was now
well over 70 and had decided to retire. Having no
children of his own to leave the farm to, he had
offered it to Dan for Peter at a very favourable price.
Alex only wanted his beer and his pipe now. He
would of course be able to help and provide advice
whenever it was needed.

Dan was still slowly coming to terms with the
news from Sarah when another unexpected letter
arrived.

Dear Dad,
   I'm really looking fwd to seeing you at Christmas.
   I've so much to tell you about Africa. I really have

learned a great deal in these last four months. I've got all sorts of ideas to make things better for these wretched people.

They have suffered from droughts for years but the new desalination plant and the channels — just like our fens – have made all the difference in the coastal regions.

I never thought I would learn the various dialects of Swahili out here but it seems that I can make myself understood with most people. Occasionally, I make a mistake. I told a story recently about seeing some ndovu swinging from branch to branch and they all burst out laughing. Later I learned that I should have used the word nyani for monkeys because ndovu are elephants!

The university is really pleased with progress and the sponsoring company have asked if I can return in the New Year and stay for at least three years! This is great news Dad so I hope you will be pleased for me.

Lots of love
Peter

Dan was sure that Peter would change his mind when he came home and heard what his dad had provided for him.

His chest had filled with pride as he explained with great pleasure his fantastic present to his son. He did not often stock champagne but Dan was convinced that the time was ripe for a celebration. He carefully opened the bottle and arranged the glasses on the coffee table in the small lounge upstairs from the bar. The horror on Peter's face telegraphed more bad news for Dan.

'Dad, I didn't ask you to do this for me,' Peter pleaded.

'I was so sure that you'd be pleased.'

'Look, Dad, I'm sorry but I just can't do this yet. I really hope you can forgive me and try to understand my point of view.'

'Peter, after all that has happened with your sister, the least I expected was some stability and common sense from you.'

'Look, Dad, please…I am begging you because I love you and I appreciate all you have done for me. But I have seen and done nothing outside my work. Before I settle down and have kids, I want to travel. For the last ten years my studies had to come first, just as you wanted. In this last year, I've visited several farms, some in Eastern Europe and recently in East Africa as you saw from my letter. I've realised how little I've travelled. And what's more how much help I could give them now I have this qualification. Besides, lots of graduates have a gap year, some even have two.'

'Oh Peter, how ungrateful can you be? You self-centred, inconsiderate, selfish boy! Do you realise what you're throwing way? Don't you care what I want?'

Peter, obviously saddened by his father's reaction, maintained a dignified but disappointed silence.

'Get out and stay out! How can you expect me to forgive you? After all I've done for you.' Dan's anger boiled and boiled and had finally overflowed. He clenched his fists, fixing in his memory the end of his dreams for his son. He lashed out with his foot, spreading the champagne all over the floor. How could he forgive him? The peace of mind he was hoping for had been smashed by the two people he cared for most in the entire world. Yet he had sent them into an exile that had created deep distress for all of them.

The night air was making his eyes water. His breath turning to a white mist as his hot breath met the frosty air. Despite the frost and snow, he realised that his face, head and arms were hot. He was perspiring profusely!

He recalled his father's advice that the strength of the human spirit is respect and open mindedness. They had both apologised and sought his forgiveness.

The failure of his human spirit was his.

Answering 'no' to every question showed a failure in human sensibility, sensitivity and, above all, respect for another's point of view. The way he had treated his children had not been the actions of a loving father. Was the road to redemption through forgiveness? Had they both been sorry and sought his forgiveness? Yes, they had! It was for him now to acknowledge that their apologies should be recognised. That old platitude about erring being human and forgiveness being divine and his failure to perform an act of goodwill at the season of goodwill, it all troubled him. They had both sought his forgiveness but he was still resisting.

In his eyes they had fallen from grace, but perhaps the greater fall could have been his own. He could no longer claim to be a loving father.

'Excuse me; do you have a room, please? Forgive me for calling so late.'

So intent had he been on reflecting on the events of the past year and on his own sense of emptiness that Dan had not noticed the stranger approaching.

The man stood in Dan's shadow, making his features difficult to see clearly. But he had hair on his face, not a long beard but enough to hide his chin. His eyes seemed to be dark pools and deep set, giving him a mildly Eastern look.

'Certainly not! What business can you have at this time of night? Shove off! Most decent folk are at home with their families!'

That word fizzed round in his mind again.

'Please forgive me for calling so late. You're not the first person to refuse me tonight! But I wish you peace.'

The stranger turned and trudged away slowly through the snow towards the hill leading away from the pub.

Dan's eyes followed his own shadow across the snow towards the hill. In the distance he could see the stranger, quite clearly now, in the glare of the lights from the porch.

But His figure threw no shadow.

Peace indeed! As he reflected on what he had just said to the stranger the realisation hit him that he had treated his own children in that same brusque and indifferent way.

The church bell struck midnight. It was Christmas, the season of goodwill – and perhaps forgiveness? Dan pondered. Had he been too harsh because they had not done his will? He thrust his head into his hands, a large lump grew in his throat and he felt the tears dribbling through his fingers. What he had shown to his children had been pride? Stupid, stupid pride.

Should he forgive?

How could he find that peace of which the stranger had spoken?

This was the tipping point.

He closed the door and resolved to ask them to come home, on their own terms. It was now his turn to provide apologies. He returned to the bar, poured a large brandy and set about making amends.

About the author

David Deanshaw has had a varied business career, initially in banking, then as a management consultant and more recently involved in the regeneration of run down town centres.

He has used his experience in writing a mixture of short stories, whilst planning on writing about situations he saw in the fields of both finance and politics. He has had several letters published in *The Times*, *Sunday Times* and *Birmingham Post* of a political and business nature.

His first novel, *The Price of Loyalty*, is based on the greed, ambition and arrogance he found watching activity in the City of London, entwined with political machinations. A sequel is being written together with a prequel involving some of the older characters.

Have you seen my husband?

Helen Combe

A nice cup of tea

Mary was pleased with herself for being so far ahead with her Christmas preparations. It was early December and she had just finished writing her last Christmas card and had dropped it with relief onto the 'done' pile.

She stretched, pushed back her chair, turned to get up and caught sight of the face pressed hard against her living room window. She let out a shriek and stood transfixed as a pair of hands came up to frame the face as it slowly scanned the room from side to side. Then it stepped back and she saw that it was a thin, elderly gentleman wearing a flat cap and a tweed jacket. He stood vacantly for a moment, then turned and headed towards the front door. There came a knocking. Mary gathered herself together and moved to open the door. The man looked exhausted and lifted his hands beseechingly.

'Have you seen my wife?' he implored.

Thoughts ran through Mary's mind. I don't know your wife, what does she look like? But she felt that this could get complicated and anyway, she hadn't seen any elderly ladies of late.

'No, I'm sorry, I haven't.'

A look of despair came over his face and he dropped his hands.

'OK, thank you,' he said, then turned and shuffled away.

Mary closed the door and hurried to the bay window to watch him as he moved to the next house, framed his hands round his face and peered through the window before heading for the door. She saw that he was wearing slippers.

The next day, Mary left her house just as her neighbour, Jean was leaving hers. Jean was a housewife, so the advantage of being at home all day, combined with a general benevolence to all mankind meant that she knew everybody and was Mary's major source of local information.

Mary cried eagerly, 'Oh Jean, I need to ask you something,' at the same time that Jean said, 'Oh Mary, I need to tell you something.'

Jean hurried across to her.

'I don't know if you've seen him, but there's an elderly gentleman who may knock on your door or look through your window.'

'Yes, that's what I was going to ask you about.'

'Well it's Mr Tomlinson, he lives on the road that backs onto ours. He's harmless. He has Alzheimer's and he's looking for his wife, but his wife passed away earlier this year.'

'Oh that's tragic.'

Mary was filled with sympathy for the old man and his constant bewildered concern for the welfare of his wife from which he could never be released.

The next evening, there was a knock at Mary's door. Mr Tomlinson stood soaked on the doorstep with rainwater pouring off the rim of his flat cap.

'Have you seen my wife?'

'No, I'm sorry. Oh look, it's pouring with rain. Why don't you come in and have a nice cup of tea?'

'Oh no, thank you. I need to find my wife.'

'Well I think you should go straight home, she's probably there wondering where you are.'

'Yes, yes, I'll do that.'

Mary closed the door and went to the window and watched him squelch across the lawn in his slippers and look through the window of the house next door. She sighed. He'd catch his death, but what could she do?

The routine continued nightly, a knock at the door at about eight o'clock, the invitation for tea and the polite refusal. Sometimes he did two or three circuits in one night.

Christmas was approaching fast and Mary was caught up in the shopping, decorating, and outings with various work colleagues and friends, so it was while she was decorating the tree that she suddenly became aware that she hadn't seen Mr Tomlinson for over week. Concerned, she hoped he was OK and even considered trying to find his house, but then thought better of it as she imagined herself looking through windows and knocking on doors and eventually crossing paths with Mr Tomlinson, on a similar mission, coming from the other direction. And if she did find him, what would she say? 'Oh, I'm so glad you're not dead'?

Anyway, he had family, she had seen him in the supermarket with a middle-aged man pushing a trolley full of food, topped with a new pair of slippers. Maybe he'd taken Mr Tomlinson home for Christmas. Mary tried to calm her conscience when there came a knock at the door, perfectly timed at eight o'clock.

'Oh thank goodness.' Mary dropped the bauble back into the box and hurried to open the door. Standing on the step was a small woman, neatly dressed in coat, boots and gloves. She had rosy cheeks, bright blue eyes and a head of curls as white as the snow that was softly tumbling from the sky.

'Excuse me, but have you seen my husband?' she asked.

Mary's jaw flapped incoherently for a moment as she struggled to connect her mouth to her brain.

'No, I'm sorry, I haven't.'

The woman cocked her head as though listening, then looked away to her right and then back again. 'Oh, it's alright, I see him. He's been getting better of late, but he still wanders off from time to time. Old habits die hard you know. So sorry to have disturbed you.' She smiled and then turned and walked away.

'That's quite alright,' Mary replied faintly. She

shut the door and then hurried to the bay window. She looked to the left but could see nothing but the gardens muffled under the snow and the street light scattering a halo of golden spangles through the ice crystals falling around it. She looked to the right and saw only the soft outlines of marshmallow cars and finally she looked to the front of the house, where a thick layer of snow lay unbroken on her garden path.

About the author
Helen Combe is a member of Solihull Writers and was shortlisted for the 'To Hull and Back' humour competition 2016. Her Facebook page HelenCombeWriter includes her short stories plus articles on her garden project and her candid, yet humorous experience of dealing with breast cancer.

Still No Room at the Inn
Dawn Knox

Coffee, black and bitter

The scruffy man hobbled down the aisle of the empty church.

He peered at the model of the chubby baby in the manger reaching up to Mary and Joseph. Everything was clean, sanitised and calm.

But it had been hot and sweaty when He was born. And crowded. Animals, relatives and well-wishers had filled the stable that His parents had been lucky to find.

The priest approached, ready to bribe the scruffy man to leave with the price of a cup of coffee.

He turned and shuffled away sadly. Even here, in this church, there was no room for Him.

About the author
Dawn's second book *The Great War, 100 stories of 100 words honouring those who lived and died 100 years ago* was published in 2016. She enjoys a writing challenge and has had stories published in various anthologies, including horror and speculative fiction, as well as romances in several women's magazines. Dawn has written a script for a play to commemorate World War One, which has been performed in her home town in Essex, as well as in Germany and France. Married with one son, she lives in Essex.

Wake-up Call

Linda Flynn

Golden Dream (a cocktail)

Catch a cliché full of illusory situations as we open the curtains to the pantomime of life…

Once upon a time, in a land far away, there was a beautiful princess, who was as fair as fair can (unnaturally) be. She was as good as she was beautiful, which in case you were wondering, was very good indeed.

Her only problem was that she required an excessive amount of beauty sleep, one hundred years to be precise.

So, when the handsome prince in tight fitting breeches found her, she was enjoying a little shut-eye.

One sight of her completely took his breath away. (To tell the truth he was also a tad breathless on account of having to hack his way through the undergrowth surrounding the castle, as a good gardener could not be found for love or money.) Which was almost as bad as wading through her massive shoe collection, in fact he nearly got himself impaled on one of her ruby slippers. But then a girl can never have too many pairs of shoes.

Anyway, to cut to the chase, the prince kissed her red, perfect Cupid's bow lips. When she could get a word in edgeways, the princess opened her big brown Bambi eyes and said, 'My Prince!' Which was perhaps a bit presumptuous and premature.

Notwithstanding, they married in haste in an intimate ceremony, with just a thousand or two honoured guests, some of whom they knew.

Certainly the blushing bride looked radiant at the side of her perfect prince, as she anticipated a life of wedded bliss in the happily ever after.

True, she had a problem or two with her mother-in-law, who would put a hard pea under the mattress of her bed and who gave her a glass slipper as a bit of a joke. She wasn't sure about all that stuff about talking to her reflection in the mirror either.

Even the prince appeared to have picked up one or two bad habits on the way. He certainly owned some beautiful things, but in her opinion he spent far too much time frantically rubbing on his magic lamp.

Of course he was entitled to own his ugly duckling and his share of furry friends, after all every dog must have his day; it was just that pushy little Puss in Boots that she couldn't stand.

Over time she began to realise that he wasn't everyone's cup of tea, particularly hers, but that there was no point in crying over spilt milk.

Nor could she really understand why the prince would insist upon climbing up her long flowing hair to reach their tower room, when there was a perfectly good spiral staircase.

On reaching the summit he would scratch his

head and mutter, 'I'm sure I came in here for something.'

It was at that point that she realised that the perfect prince she had married had turned into a flipping frog.

The best that she could hope for was to wake up and discover that it had all been just a dream.

About the Author

Linda Flynn has had two humorous novels published: *Hate at First Bite* for 7-9 year-olds, and *My Dad's a Drag* for teenagers. Both won Best First Chapter in The Writers' Billboard competition.

She has six educational books with the Heinemann Fiction Project. In addition she has written for a number of newspapers and magazines, including theatre reviews and several articles on dogs.

Her short stories with Bridge House include: five adult stories: *To Take Flight,* in the *Going Places* anthology, *I knew it in the Bath*, in *Something Hidden, Snowdrop* in the anthology *Snowflakes, All That Glitters...* in the *Baubles* collection, *The Litter in Glitter* in the Christmas 17 anthology *Gliterary Tales*, as well as *The Wild Ones* for teenagers, in *Devils, Demons and Werewolves*. Two children's short stories: *The Secret Messenger* and *Timid Tim* were included in *Hippo-Dee-Doo-Dah*.

Linda's website is: www.lindaflynn.com

Chimes at Midnight
Paula R C Readman

Chilli chocolate and red wine

I cross the wide expanse of the lawn at the front of Crowhurst Hall; a journey I've made many times before. However, this time it feels different.

High above me the hunter's moon casts its lengthy shadows as the first flurries of the season snowfall, swirling around me, whipped up by the bitter wind. Tugging at the fabric of my skirt it seems to sweep me up and carries me over the threshold of my home.

In the cold hallway I stand dressed in what was once my finery before the old long-case clock, studying its delicate, ornate hands. In the past, as a child, I found them fascinating too, but then they marked the passing of a happier time. Now as I watch the seconds tick away, I wait for its hourly chime, but they do not come.

Evoking some half-remembered remark, I recall the past and the present like the sweeping hands of a clock run together. Yet, it seems like only yesterday when I heard it ring out its melancholy chimes to mark my passing. They resonated around my ice-cold body before the soil fell clattering upon my coffin lid as the mourners left me beneath the frosty ground.

Now the only sound I hear is the ticking of the clock as I wonder what has disturbed the tranquillity of my eternal slumber.

I know I cannot remain for long within these walls for I'm no longer welcome. He who robbed me of everything I held so dear would be outraged to know I've returned once more.

My faded, black taffeta skirt rustles on the stone tiled floors as I move aimlessly around. For a moment I linger in the library as wisps of tenebrous memories come flooding back.

Suddenly I'm aware of some unfinished business, which may account for my homecoming. Climbing the marble staircase I pause; resting my hand lightly on its carved banister. Glancing up I see the gentle smiling faces of my beloved parents whom, with vacant, painted eyes stare back at me.

As I reminisce about their untimely passing, something cold creeps across the back of my bony neck and shoulders making me shudder. I brush my fingertips across my icy cheek longing to feel unshed tears washing my face with warmth as I cry for what was once mine.

I enter my old dressing room and find that the chilling night air fills it with dampness. Prior to my death my servant, Annie, would've made sure a welcoming fire filled it with warmth and light, but now it's as welcoming as a cold, empty grave.

In the past, I would've sat before the large ornate

mirror, with its exquisite carvings of cherubs, love hearts, and doves, combing my glossy, golden tresses while dreaming of my darling Henry's return from London.

I recall too how my heart leapt with pleasure on hearing the sound of his carriage on the cobbles outside my window, knowing soon in his embrace I would hear his sweet, whispered words of love.

Now seated before it all I see is bone-dry, cadaverous skin stretching across my emaciated face as I brush dirt and worms from all that remain of my hair.

Has time passed me by so quickly that I'm nothing, but bones?

The sound of the door catch lifting brings me out of my reverie and I dissolve into the shadows as a young girl, just ripening into womanhood glides into the room.

Crossing the pool of moonlight she heads in my direction.

Her beauty astounds me.

With raven-black hair, she's clothed only in a long, white nightgown, her bare feet blue with cold. She moves around the room with exaggerated movements while opening and closing the drawers and cupboard doors. In her dream-like state, she seems to be searching for something.

'How could he betray me so?' she mutters.

Stepping out of the shadows, I whisper, 'Hello,

young beauty, I wonder, did I disturb your slumber?'

Though her tear-stained eyes are unblinking, something flickers across her forlorn face makes me realise that, unlike me, death has no claim on her, but something disturbs the noctambulist's sleep.

I follow her, but she shows no signs that she's conscious of me.

'Please, do not be afraid. I mean you no harm. What disturbs your sleep?' I ask.

She turns, her golden eyes dart back and forth as though seeking out a sound.

Aah, she does not see me, but hears me.

She lifts her left hand to brush a strand of her raven hair from her lips when something shimmers in the moonlight.

'What's this you're wearing?' I raise my bony, dust-dry hand before her face so she can see what hangs on my fleshless finger. 'It's a ring? So he's wed another, making us three?' I say as my heart breaks, knowing I've failed again.

Bewilderment settles on her face as her eyes begin to dilate, I realise then she sees me as a dream. Her soft voice carries neither weight nor sound, like a child's sleeping breath, she asks, 'Who are you?'

'I'm Eleanor,' I say 'I'm back from whence I slept so peacefully to warn you. Though I've failed another I once tried to save. Fate was so cruel.'

Her young brow creases as she stares right

through me, then, as if she's suddenly aware that I'm standing there.

She steps back. Her hand flies to her mouth to stifle a cry. With trembling lips, she utters, 'Incubus, Succubus, be gone!'

In contempt, I shake my shrunken head as dirt, worms, and hair falls from me scattering around my bony feet.

'I am neither. You may have youth and beauty on your side, but your days are numbered. As you see me standing before you, so you shall be one day. For there's no escaping from the hands of time. I wish only to see you grow old and not die before time has lined your face.'

Suddenly the sound of the tolling clock echoes with the passing of another hour.

'At last,' I cry, holding out my fleshless arms as the mournful chimes resound through the sleeping house, and the ravages of time are undone.

I stand clothed once more, flesh upon flesh, muscle, and sinew. Time restores my golden blonde tresses, but I cannot linger. Vanity is a weakness for living as time isn't mine.

She too wakes into half-sleep and whispers, 'You're Lady Eleanor. I've seen your portrait, and your tomb in the cemetery. Five years have passed since you were murdered by an unknown intruder while your husband was away.'

'What tale is this? Come; let me show you the

truth, for it too will be your fate, if you aren't careful.'

'Not the truth!' With a shudder, she hurries to her bedroom.

I follow her in fear she'll wake him.

In my haste I step into her bedroom. I'm surprised to find how little has changed. All that we selected together for our love nest he now shares with another.

Wiping her tears, the noctambulist stares down at her sleeping husband.

'Fear not, he sleeps,' say I.

She glances in my direction, her lower lip trembles as she whispers, 'When I see him sleeping so peacefully, my heart is full of love. The way the curls of his black hair fall lightly on his ruddy cheek. See how his lips part as he breathes gently. See the line of his jaw, so strong. How could you not fall for such a man?'

I laugh, 'Sweet nightwalker, if you heart is full of so much love for this sleeping man, then what makes you roam alone while he sleeps so serenely?'

A questioning look flickers across her innocent face, 'Should I not fear you, Lady Eleanor, for am I not talking in my disturbed sleep with a ghost?'

'I'm not here to do you harm. The living should not fear us who've passed over. We can do you no injury, sweet child. There's one who is living that you need to fear far more.'

'How can I trust you, you who have no right to be here?'

'Let me join you in your nocturnal amble through my home. For I was a child here…'

'This much I know,' say she.

'What troubles you so?'

She gestures to the room, 'There was another who called this house her home, but unlike you, she's not a ghost.'

'Come; let's go where we can talk more freely.'

As the noctambulist leaves, her husband rolls over. I feel the darkness within the room rearrange itself as I wait for him to awake so I can peer into his dark, soulless green eyes once more, but he sleeps on.

In the hallway, apart from the steady ticking of the clock, the only other sound is that of the noctambulist's bare feet on the stone floor as we enter the library.

As though she's fully awake, she crosses to the fireplace and adds another log to the dying embers. With a crackle, the fresh dry wood ignites throwing its warmth and light around the room, but although its heat cannot warm my dry bones, I still shudder as the shadows of my past gathered in every corner waiting for me to tell my tale of betrayal.

'Please can you tell me about the other woman?' I ask, though I fear the worst. For I had visited her on such a night, at least three years ago, to warn her the best I could that death would be at her door. Unlike this noctambulist, the second wife did not have a strong constitution.

On that night before the clock struck the hour to restore me, I had stepped out of the shadows too early and she had gazed upon my worm eaten face. Her pitiful screams woke what was left of her household.

Standing at the French windows, the sleepwalker has her back to me, staring at the moon through the lightly falling snow.

She turns and with a heavy sigh saying, 'My husband has no right to marry me when he has a wife who lives in a mental asylum. I uncovered Lady Helen's journal in the library and read about her fear of destitution. Her fears slowly descended her into madness. Unlike me, she was not strong, when Henry left her alone for days to travel to London. She feared he wouldn't return. All too soon, the servants deserted her. With no money to pay them their wages, she roamed the icy corridors alone.

'Now you appeared, haunting me in my dreams… Oh, why do I doubt the man I love so true?'

'Do you not believe her?' I ask, on hearing the hesitation in her voice. 'Once I was like you believing every word he uttered. Now I am, but a ghost belonging to the borderland. Like Lady Helen and you, he deceived me too. Not for love he married me, but my father's money. The day he drove the knife into my beating heart, he took pleasure in telling me so.'

'Were you not killed by an unknown hand?' she asks, puzzlement lining her clear complexion.

'No. The hand that took my life was none other than that of my husband, Henry. In this very room, he drove in his knife taking such delight in telling me how he'd taken my parents' lives too, by having their carriage driven off the road. He'd discovered that my father had made inquiries in London's high society, finding out that among the gambling set Henry was notorious for being in debt.

With my dying breath, I cursed him. That's why I'm not free to sleep for eternity, until he has paid his debts in full to me.'

'Oh, it's all true,' she sobs, 'he married me for my money too. While he has been away, I uncovered his secrets here in the library. I found Lady Helen's journal and a bloodied knife. I wanted so much to know the truth,' Noctambulist whispers with a heavy-heart.

She crosses to a shelf. Half-hidden in shadows, pulls out a jewelled handled knife, and lays it before me.

'It's the knife,' I utter, 'with which he took my life.'

Suddenly, the library door bursts open and Henry steps in. On seeing the noctambulist sitting alone, he booms, 'Oh, I do declare, my new wife betrays me not with another, but I feel madness fills the air yet again.' Laughing, he continued, 'Am I so cursed to find that another I took to be my bride suffering from lunacy too.'

I whisper to the noctambulist, 'Dear lady, pray take your leave. The time has come to set us free. Take Lady Helen's journal and keep it safe. Sleep deeply now until daybreaks.'

Picking up the book, the noctambulist turns her back on Henry, and takes her leave without a word.

He goes to follow, but the door slams shut. Watching in horror, he sees the key spin in the lock and vanishes.

'What trickery is this?' he cries in surprise.

Then out of the shadows, I appear still beautiful in a dark unnatural way, as I was on the day he took my life.

'None that I can see, my Lord, but revenge for those you've betrayed with your lies.' Laughing, I lift the knife, 'An eye for an eye.'

His eyes widen with fear as the cold of the grave radiates from me. His face pales as he raises his trembling hands as if to protect himself.

'This cannot be; you're a ghost that I should not see. Dear God, help me and send this devil back to the ground where she should be.'

The French windows burst open as the fire goes out. Shadows draw around him with a sudden lurch;

he drops to the ground. Protruding from his chest, the bejewelled knife immersed in his cold, black heart.

I stand over him as his confused spirit begins to rise.

Staring down at his dying self, he whispers, 'What have you done to me?'

'Time to pay for your sins. Now come follow me,' I turn towards the open doors.

'You cannot do this to me! I'm still breathing and can be saved,' he screams. With a wave of my hand, he has no choice and reluctantly trails after me.

We cross the lawn to the cemetery. In the freshly fallen snow, only his footprints will be seen by everyone when the new day breaks.

In the distance, I hear the old hall clock ring out its melancholy chimes for the passing of the hour as the old day becomes the new. I sink into my grave, dragging with me what remained of Henry's conscious self, down to lay at my side.

Suddenly aware of his surroundings, Henry turns to face me, just as the worms slither back into my eye sockets, nostrils, mouth, and hair as time takes back what it had restored to me. His scream fills our narrow space.

'Oh, such joys at last to have you here beside me in this cold ground, dearest Henry. Did you think you could escape our wedding vows? Let no man put asunder not even death could keep us part.'

As I slip peacefully into eternal sleep with my husband at my side, the tombstone above our head now tells the truth; 'An unknown intruder murdered us who lie beneath this cold, cold ground'.

About the Author
Paula R C Readman has won two short story competitions one which was the Harrogate Crime Writing competition, when Mark Billingham picked her story as the overall winner. She has also been published by English Heritage, Parthian Books and Bridge House in their anthologies. To find out more about her writing:
paulareadman1.wordpress.com

Christmas on the High Street
Dawn Knox

Unsweetened cranberry juice – seasonal but bitter and harsh

Like a rock in a river, he stood, while shoppers flowed around him, their faces resolute and haunted. No one acknowledged him. Their eyes darted this way and that, as they sought the quickest route into each shop.

Well, there was so much to do on Christmas Eve.

A young girl stopped in front of him and looked up silently, with questioning eyes, before her mother seized her hand and dragged her back into the crowd.

They'd celebrate his birthday tomorrow or that's what they would claim to be doing. In reality, they didn't want to know him at all.

About the Author

Dawn's second book *The Great War, 100 stories of 100 words honouring those who lived and died 100 years ago* was published in 2016. She enjoys a writing challenge and has had stories published in various anthologies, including horror and speculative fiction, as well as romances in several women's magazines. Dawn has written a script for a play to commemorate World War One, which has been performed in her home town in Essex, as well as in Germany and France. Married with one son, she lives in Essex.

Let it Snow

Alan Cadman

JD and Coke

Henry usually hated the white stuff, bad for business, but not if it fell on Christmas Eve. Last minute shoppers drifted in and out of the tube station as he strapped on his guitar. He knew if he played seasonal songs, with added snow as a bonus, more money would be gifted to him. He glanced towards the leaden sky. Bring it on. This could be pay day.

Not everyone was full of good cheer. An elderly man, in a well-worn overcoat, jabbed at him with a walking stick. 'You bloody scrounger, why don't you get a proper job like I had to?'

Henry ignored him, rubbed the palms of his hands together, sang something about the weather outside being so frightful. He carried on with a few more cheesy tunes before switching to an old rock ballad.

'Oh, I love this song. It takes me right back to when I was a teenager.'

Shocked by the enthusiastic voice, Henry nearly fell off his fold-up stool. At any other time of the year, commuters didn't normally stop to make complimentary comments. Most of them hurried past, turned their heads, or dropped some loose change. This one remained in the same position, with a puzzled look spreading across her face.

In front of him stood a middle-aged woman; laden with bags of various colours. She moved closer to him. 'You sing it well. Your voice is so like the original, just a little deeper perhaps.'

Henry gave her his best smile; this one should be good for a couple of quid.

The woman snapped her fingers as if she had discovered something remarkable. 'You *are* him. Those blue eyes of yours will always have the same twinkle.'

He stopped playing and scratched three days of white stubble on his chin. 'You're getting me mixed up with someone else, love, and no I'm not Santa Claus.'

'I remember seeing you on Top of the Pops in the nineteen seventies. You came on last after Rod Stewart and David Essex. Number one in the charts for two weeks you were.'

He remained silent, twisted a tuning peg.

'I had pictures of you on my bedroom wall. I bought all your records until you vanished off the radar, so to speak.' She paused to catch her breath. 'I remember that Christmas concert you did. I'd loved to have gone. I never got to see you in the flesh… well, not until now of course.'

Henry stuffed his hands into his pockets.

'I've always wanted your autograph.' She found one of her till receipts then fished around in her pockets for a pen. 'Can you sign this for me, please?'

He sighed, took them from her, and scribbled something down.

'That's your real name. When I watched you on the telly, you weren't called that.' She gave him another scrap of paper.

He tried again.

'I knew it. You're the one and only, Bobby Balsamo.' While pressing a ten pound note into his hand, she frowned and peered closely at his face. 'What happened, Bobby?'

He shrugged his shoulders. 'I just got caught up in a rock 'n' roll lifestyle. Some can handle it, others… well, you know.' When she pulled out her phone, he added, 'Please, no selfies.'

'OK, no problem, but will you do me a favour?'

He raised his eyebrows. Even though he hadn't started playing his guitar again, a few more coins rattled by his feet. He mouthed a 'thank you' towards a man who had made the donation; grateful he had more compassion than that miserable one earlier.

'Bobby,' the woman said, 'will you play your number one single again just for me?'

'Haven't you got any more shopping to do?'

'Please, it will be the best Christmas present ever.'

He shifted in his seat; avoided looking at her. A few flakes of snow descended; sticking on anything in their way. The grimy cityscape was about to turn white.

'Bobby?'

For the first time in nearly forty years, he no longer felt like Henry Smith. Snow began falling heavier. Umbrellas were raised; scarves wrapped tighter. Bobby Balsamo stood up and looked straight at his audience of one. He hesitated then strummed the opening bars of his most famous song.

About the author:

Alan has been writing short stories for ten years. In 2011 he made the short list for one story and was a prize winner for flash fiction. He also won first prize, of £100, in a poetry competition in 2013. The three accolades were awarded by the best-selling UK magazine for writers. His work has been read out on Internet radio, and published in hard copy magazines and e-zines.

An Affair in A-Z

Lisa Williams

An illicit coffee when you should be working

A child full of Autumn sun, not perturbed by the gathering storm, makes them with giggle tinged breath and an urgently dipped stick.

Gliding magical mirrored globes.

Float towards a fuscous sky.

They rise. Drift.

Reflecting a violet wing over a chalk hill. Remains of an impromptu picnic. A hand held, just a little too long, on the tartan check. They see the glance. The colouring of that cheek that he slides his against. To whisper in her ear. They see the beginning of something but keep their secrets safe as with a quick liquid burst they are gone.

Beginnings often catch us unaware.

The whisper almost lost in the folding of the picnic blanket. Trapped in its tartan folds and packed away for winter.

But she catches it with a gasp before it creeps along her spine. Turns to check she's heard it right as an obsidian curtain drops, the rain starts and the ground sighs at its touch.

With arms outstretched the child flies down the hill. Leaving them in the rain. Holding a blanket. A decision hanging in the air. Thunder then, rumbles its approach as a flutter of beating wings rise from a distant tree.

Crisp leaves carpet the path as they stroll. Just the two of them although decorum walks between them as they both battle the inner need to be so much closer.

Midas had run on ahead touching the few leaves that still stubbornly clung to bare branches before heading home to write summer's eulogy.

Moments ago this day had stretched out endlessly before them but now the streetlights come on and draw it to an unwelcome close. They kiss then in the glowing embers of their first shared day.

A kiss tinged with coffee.

And a promise of so much more

December didn't bring the expected chill to their trysts. It sent them inside and as they left uncharted waters and made for land a fear of discovery silently crept behind them. Detection by those that shouldn't ever know of those broken promises, the stolen happiness they'd shared together.

Their heartbeats quickened by more than simply desire. They met with pockets full of excuses for the questions that never came. Deleted messages, plans not on any calendar; until they met it was as if they didn't even exist.

They became an ephemeral whisper of broken vows on winter's sharp easterly wind.

Each passing day they spoke. Surreptitiously. Shared the time when they could, hidden from prying eyes. And from this, deep within them it grew. An all-encompassing build of desire. A need. Not felt before. Nurtured it seemed from nothing.

Hopes, held together with gossamer thin strands. They tiptoed to keep them tied tight, tried not to rock their boat, neither wanting their tenuous bond to break whilst on their trip.

They fed each other's hunger with this fresh found joy. With the thrill of excitement they wanted to shout from the rooftops but which was too secret to share.

Firelit curves only give a glimpse of the picture on the fur rug. It's a Tuesday afternoon early in December. The air is breath-catchingly cold.

There's a trail of recklessly discarded clothes from the hall. Edges define then in the warming glow after a frenzied undressing. As two shapes lean together, reach forward and the curves meet to join as one. That fireside kiss needs both hands to still her shiver of delight.

Firelit curves that move gently, rocking to a

backdrop of gasped breath and the smell of cedar and red wine are perhaps easier to make out.

Grey skies are hidden by a curtain pulled closed in the daytime. He becomes her sunshine on brumous days. They draw closer. In embraces longed for since their last meet. She flicks the Christmas tree lights on with a bare toe, the only illumination in the room.

This closed door togetherness, one they can't share in public provides a frisson that they don't really need.

A turn.

A look.

A coming together until they're so close a marriage certificate couldn't come between them.

And then.

Their kisses.

That feed their aches of desire and seemingly erase all time before them.

Have you ever longed for escape?

For something new and exciting to take hold?

They hadn't courted this. But there it was. Found when they hadn't been searching. They didn't feel they could control this need, urgency almost, to be together.

Over Christmas assignations were harder to arrange with a surfeit of family filling the house. A shared afternoon before, he unwrapped her, they had their celebration then. Then used the time to try and halt things. Hoping common sense would take over.

Tell-tale footprints led to his door though, when the year ended covered in a blanket of snow.

Icicles like frosted alabaster outside the upstairs window mirror the honey drip of pleasure from within as the New Year starts with a warming fervour. Forced apart over Yule their aches desperately need sating. With a wife visiting relatives they take advantage on a neatly made marital bed.

Wrong.

So very wrong.

But from the guttural groan from behind the bedroom door followed by a tremulous 'YES' they have found solace in each other's arms. Needs met. That dull pain of desire gratifyingly quelled. The year continues as they grasp fleeting moments of joy together in an otherwise calamitous world.

Joy.

Unbridled joy.

Rippling through life is a rarity. And when it's found it needs to be nurtured, kept safe. Lest it rise on the wind and fly to warmer shores. And so they look after their bliss as Spring brings with it pendulous clumps of blossom that falls on their heads like confetti.

Confetti. Like at the weddings they'd both had but not to each other. The words unspoken, they shared that though. They'd both married the wrong person.

Fresh hope burst from the ground beneath where they sat. Fingers entwined. Susurrations of nothings between them, peppered with kisses.

Kisses.

Endless kisses. That both feed the ache and sate in one delicious mouth aching paradox. Concealed usually from view for no one to know. Stolen on a busy street. Risky, but necessary. Caught up in the kilig, a bounce in steps. The monotony of life suddenly easier to bear with this secret burst of bliss tucked away in their hearts.

The anticipation that escalates with each passing day apart, for the next time. Snatched seconds of a call. A text. A chance meeting.

Making do with memories of a lip brushing softly against flesh until the inevitable next time.

Lost loves can always be found if they want to be.

The deep plummeting sadness of being apart, without contact feels like it could kill. The hurt, the sadness takes over and eats into the day with a heavy dark bite.

She sits alone at her table. Marmalade on toast catching in her throat as the memories rise to the surface with a sparkle that fades as soon as they surface. There's no escape from them. Her skin tingles with the remembrance of his kisses and the tears almost rust her heart.

He hopes she knows he's thinking of her.

Magic, like lightning can strike the same place more than once, and so it did in her heart as spring turned to summer and he returned. She'd mourned for what they'd shared in the week he was away. Tried to tell herself he wasn't hers to lose. But as he came back from foreign shores, a little tanned, he had a deeper hunger in his eyes.

They kissed in the street.

Discovery would stop them having to hide.

And with the door barely closed they came together like a battle. Fighting away the week apart with an almost spellbinding fury.

No one knowing about something can feel strange. The more it goes on. Ethereal and dreamlike can become just plain weird. But it was hard to reveal something that was just for them. And so many others would be hurt by the pleasure they shared.

So they chose to keep it safe for now, although it meant there was so much they couldn't do together. The simple normalities. A morning. Brushing teeth. Even a supermarket shop somehow held a tantalising tug of desire.

We always want what we haven't got, they had each other, but neither liked having to share.

Only when you've had an affair can you know that heart clutch, lurch of panic when you're at last discovered.

A tell-tale receipt left in the car, singing in the shower, vestiges of scent on a dress. Being spotted walking out of the cinema on a Thursday afternoon by a friend. The pocketful of excuses had tumbled unnoticed under the seat with the popcorn as they kissed.

Both blinking in the light, questions hit them unaware. Their kiss flushed faces give them away. Prompting a phone call later. A third degree. Hurt that this huge secret hadn't been a shared one.

Paris. A balcony. A bare shoulder.

Bubbles of excitement rise inside them like in a flute of champagne. A secret shared meant they could spread their wings. Cover stories provide a night away, a whole night together.

They are bowled over by possibilities of the enchanted evening ahead. More time than they've ever known before. And a romantic new city to explore.

They choose the nearest supermarket.

And a trolley. To make it seem more real.

Later as stars sparkle burning their last through the window they sit up in bed with biscuits and marshmallows. Giggling with adventure and delights.

Quelled feelings build. Good or bad. The feeling between them had built and built and had to explode. In a Paris hotel room they saw the future. This was it. Now. It wasn't going to get better.

Neither would leave their partner. Children. Complications. The house. There was a tower of reasons hovering over them. But, as they slid down the bed to spend their first night together, on a layer of biscuit crumbs it didn't matter.

Their happiness was here. Was on a hill. Was wherever they could be, regardless of who they shared the rest of life with.

Rising early the next morning because of open curtains they do try to make it seem normal. But just having the head on the next pillow to wake up to seemed strange. They both sat up, as reality sank in. Thoughts naturally going those they usually woke up next to with a swift lurch of guilt.

They reassure each other.

And then slip into each other's arms and reassure each other without words.

It was a one off. To be enjoyed but possibly never to be repeated.

But a little bit of wanting it to be forever had crept in.

She wakes with an emptiness the next morning. Looks across at a pillow without him on it and heads straight for the shower, unable to face her husband. Needing to wash her flesh that had been so kissed and loved

The emptiness grows as the day goes on. Niggles. Arguments. Little life battles that her other life didn't have. She knew it was too good to be true that it was a dream not reality.

Could never be.

As the argument continues into the afternoon she feels lucky to be able to visit that alternate hedonistic universe, share some pleasure.

The problem he had was that he just wanted her. That was it.

Needed to have her, completely. Her way of seeing things, the delight of the new. He couldn't see the solution though and he didn't like that. He was a man for which solutions came easily.

His wife was away.

Paris.

And the house seemed no emptier than usual. Her not being here didn't matter, it was missing some laughter. It needed the warmth and fun that he'd found away from his marriage.

He reached for a drink as he sat down to think about all the options.

Ultimately you may judge our couple.

Their indiscretions.

Their selfish need to squirrel away seeking pleasure, lack of concern for other's feelings in the quest to satisfy their uncontrollable urges.

You may cloud the story with a tale of your own. It's inevitable. It's the nature of narrative, but this one's mine, or theirs that I'm telling for them.

And if I can confide a secret here, now that we've bonded, it's not just the tale of two, a single couple. It's their partners too, unified in their scandalous encounters. So they deserve each other despite not wanting each other.

Vestige of a distant scent. Perfume. A strange sillage on the air. Just enough to jangle nerves but she wonders if it's in her mind. Sullied by her own misdemeanours

A trepidation to mention, less it prompts a barrage of questions. Where were you? (With him) and she doesn't want that to spoil the joy he's built up earlier for her.

So she ignores it. Like the other little suggestions that her husband's cheating on her. Although deep down she's beginning to realise she's coming second best in both relationships. A truth that hurts more than anything else ever could.

When wishes come true.

What's left then?

What happens to our dreams, a tumble of reveries redundant as we reach tranquillity, our Arcadia on those serene lapis seas?

That bumble bee buzz of contentment.

Can it last forever? Or will we seek new idylls?

She wonders if he said he'd leave his wife. Would that be it? Or is it a never ending circle. And in a decade or so do we begin again with a new brittle litany. Slip into yet another dream world.

Will he repeat and in turn leave her?

And so continue into a perpetual ammonites spiral.

X A single kiss at the end of a text. That in itself wasn't unusual but she stared at it longer than she normally would. Before it plummeted into the chasm of deleted texts.

Evidence erased. Often before the message has sunk in. But this. A small flickering screen in a shaking hand.

Tomorrow The Zoo Meet you in the car park. Bring C X

Another car park. But to take Charlie? It seemed strange. She couldn't know the depth of the meaning but with a tremor in her heart she mulled before a call took her away and back to reality.

'You know I'll never leave her.' It was murmured into her neck almost like another whisper long ago. Another couple. Another affair. Almost went unheard because of the huge crack of her heart breaking.

A magpie landed in the park, followed by another.

Two for joy.

'I know,' she said hiding her sadness.

I hoped I was wrong. I wanted to be more. I needed you to be mine. Please leave her. I thought we made each other happy. She didn't say, swallowed the words down deeper below her aching heart as one magpie disappeared with an iridescent green flash.

Zoos are the perfect places to visit when you've got to keep a secret; full of school trips and tired parents of toddlers.

No one there to hover over you, overhear you saying that you're leaving her. No pressure, but it should make things easier.

And as an excited toddler watches a tiger pace up and down in his corroded cage, a burst ball in his mouth they hold each other tight.

And she rests a cheek on his. Knowing that from

this inevitably sad ending something good has definitely just begun for them.

Maybe for all of them.

About the author
Lisa Williams. Domestic slattern. Obsessive reader. Writes a bit.

www.noodlebubble.co.uk

Schrödinger's Data Stick

Helen Combe

Caffè corretto

'Boil, damn you!'

Milo shook his fist at the kettle. He was gasping for a cup of coffee, especially now that he had the stress of a quantum entangled cat in a state of limbo, howling, snarling and rampaging around in the box on his kitchen table.

Milo liked to occupy himself by recreating experiments, and the simplicity of Schrödinger's had always appealed, combined with the complexity of getting his hands on a fragment of plutonium and a phial of cyanide. Knowing that the police were currently executing a countrywide hunt for him just added to the excitement. However the experiment itself was proving to be a lot less satisfying than the preparation.

'Boil you bastard!' He yelled at the kettle.

Schrödinger's experiment was actually theoretical, designed to illustrate the problem with the Copenhagen interpretation of quantum mechanics. The cat is supposed to be simultaneously alive and dead, as a result of a quantum subatomic event that may or may not occur. Specifically, an atom of the plutonium may decay, causing the phial to shatter and so kill the cat. Alternatively, the atom may not decay, the phial will not shatter and the cat will live. However until the box is opened and the contents are observed, the cat will be simultaneously alive and dead, a state referred to as quantum superposition. Once the box is opened, reality collapses into one possibility or the other and the cat is only then definitely alive and kicking or sadly deceased.

Aiming another snarl at the obstinately humming kettle, Milo picked up his data stick in order to record his observation that the state of feline quantum superposition is a surprisingly noisy one. He inserted the data stick into the USB port. It didn't fit. He turned it over and reinserted it. It still didn't fit. He turned it over yet again and it still refused to fit.

'Christ, I need a coffee!' he howled.

'Yarroogghh! Gah! Spit!' complained the superannuated (or not) cat.

Milo reversed the data stick and looked at it. The USB connector had until then been in a state of quantum superposition, neither up nor down, but now that Milo had observed it, reality collapsed into one possibility and the connector assumed the position of 'Up'.

'Bloody data stick, you do it to me every time,' he wailed.

It did do it every time, because the proof of the entanglement theory was there in front of him several times every day, without the need to murder a cat (or not).

In fact, the world is full of everyday truths that are known, yet completely ignored, and every rule is proved by its exception. Milo knew the old saying that a watched pot never boils, but he didn't believe it. In fact, the pot was the exception to the rule of quantum entanglement. While it was observed, it remained in a state of neither boiled nor unboiled.

'Yowowowwll!' cried the undead moggy.

'Oh for God's sake!'

Milo ripped the box open and the cat shot out over his shoulder. The cat had in fact never been in a state of quantum entanglement. Observation does not have to be visual, it can also be auditory. The plutonium however, had been caught between states, but upon being observed, reality collapsed into one of two possibilities. The plutonium atom decayed, the phial of cyanide shattered and released its poisonous vapour. Milo observed, breathed, gasped and crumpled to the floor.

The kettle, the exception to the rule, finding itself no longer observed, was released from its state of quantum entanglement and quickly came to a roiling boil.

About the author
Helen Combe is a member of Solihull Writers and was shortlisted for the 'To Hull and Back' humour competition 2016. Her Facebook page HelenCombeWriter includes her short stories plus articles on her garden project and her candid, yet humorous experience of dealing with breast cancer.

Sport for Fun

Roger Noons

A pint of bitter shandy – to start with

I didn't cry the first time my nose was broken on the rugby field, but when the Games Master pushed a finger up each nostril and squeezed, the tears began to flow. I was even more regretful in detention the following afternoon. 'You shouldn't have called Mr Davies a bastard,' my Form Teacher advised.

When I played Old Boys' rugby, the nose treatment became a not uncommon event. There was always at least one doctor in the team and often another watching. My worst experience of injury was holding a fellow player still while his ear was sewn back on.

About the Author
Roger Noons is a regular contributor to CaféLit, wowing us with many 100 worders and some longer ones – and you can also read his stories in our *Best of CaféLit* series.

Green for Danger

Penny Rogers

Gin and angostura bitters

The atmosphere in Stephanie's lounge crackled. The two women had never found each other's company particularly easy, and now they scarcely tolerated each other. On her 60th birthday, Kayla decided it was time to bury the hatchet with Stephanie, who was after all, her only relation.

So Kayla emailed to ask if she could visit, and received a curt reply indicating that Stephanie would be available at 3.15 on the day suggested.

The interior of her cousin's house was just as she remembered it, tasteful and very dull. Kayla refused to take off her shoes as she sashayed into the lounge. Stephanie, muttering about heels ruining the solid oak floor, did not immediately notice the occupant of the shoes homing-in on the mantelpiece.

'Darling, where did you get this beauty?' Kayla's eyes fell upon Stephanie's treasure, a small green horse that she had found in a car boot sale. 'It's jade. I have one that matches exactly. A pair is worth so much more than just one. Can we do a deal?'

'No. We can't both own the pair, and I'm happy just having one,' snapped Stephanie. Kayla shrugged her shoulders and left immediately after tea. Stephanie was suspicious, so in anticipation of a follow-up visit she hid the figurine and found a plastic imitation on eBay to replace it.

She never saw either horse again; neither did she see the green Audi that knocked her down. Kayla overcame her grief by organising the disposal of Stephanie's belongings, though she gave up as soon as she found the jade horse.

About the author

Penny writes short stories, flash fiction and poetry. She has been published in anthologies including *Henshaw One* and *Two, This Little World* and *The Best of CaféLit 5* as well as in *Bare Fiction, Writers' Forum* and *South.*

https://pennyrogers.wordpress.com

Clean Breaks

Roger Noons

A pint of brown and mild

The nurse had left the curtain open so I watched Belinda talking to the doctor. He touched her arm as he explained the prognosis. Five minutes later, she was by my side.

'He says it's a clean break. It will mend and you'll be able to play again.'

Four days later, she collected me and drove me home. As soon as I was settled, she told me it was over. A clean break would be best for both of us.

That was last season. I push myself in training, praying that Dr Ruston also plays rugby for a local team.

About the Author
Roger Noons is a regular contributor to CaféLit, wowing us with many 100 worders and some longer ones – and you can also read his stories in our *Best of CaféLit* series.

Ruby

Lisa Williams

A cup of tea in bed

Geoff always woke promptly without an alarm clock and immediately mourned for the one he married. He rose and she stared up at him. Smiling. Not a care in the world. From their wedding photo, taken exactly forty years ago to the day.

He washed, dressed. Thinking that they could be celebrating today. A big family party in a balloon filled hall.

Happiness.

Joy.

After a lifetime of shared bliss.

He sighed and took her up a cup of tea in bed. Hoping today would be a reasonable day for her. And that she'd at least recognise who he was.

About the author
Lisa Williams. Domestic slattern. Obsessive reader. Writes a bit.

www.noodlebubble.co.uk

The Visitors

Jenny Palmer

A blueberry smoothie

There were two of them last time. My house is just about the right size for one visitor at a time. When there are two, it is a bit of a tight squeeze. Trips to the bathroom are difficult. Timing is all important. I usually give up my bedroom and sleep in the spare room, which doubles up as a study. It is full of books. There are so many ideas floating around in there that I find it difficult to switch off. In the mornings, I feel shattered but still feel duty-bound to ask the visitors how they have slept even though I already know the answer. They have got the best room in the house.

I first started doing Air B&B for a bit of extra cash. Then I found I liked the company. You can get lonely living out here, with only the sheep to talk to and the birds. I don't usually get involved with the guests. I prefer to leave them to their own devices. I told them to be sure and bring their walking shoes. I live out in the sticks, five miles from the nearest town. The bus service is poor. To go anywhere, they have to walk. I prefer it if the visitors go out during the day. But the weather was against them. It rained all week and the ground was too muddy to walk on.

It would have been a struggle for them to buy in food. There was no way they would be have been able to carry it home. The bus stop is at least half an hour away. So, they came with me when I went shopping. In the end, we decided to cook together. I enjoy trying out new recipes. They were fond of using super foods like quinoa and blueberries. It made a change from my normal diet.

They said it was overcrowded where they came from. You couldn't move without bumping into people. They were looking for a place with more space. They wanted to know what it was like living in the countryside. They were interested in the history of the place.

So, one day, I suggested we visit the local museum. It has been done up recently with lottery money and gone all touchy-feely with sound recordings of bird calls and local accents. But there are some good displays and, if you follow it through, you can trace the history of mankind from pre-historic times right to the present.

Another day I took them to a textile museum, where they could see the original machines working, just as they had done during the industrial revolution. The noise was deafening but they loved it. They had never seen anything like it and took video footage to show back home. On the strength of that, I took them to the nearby abbey, where Cistercian monks had once laboured, cultivating crops, rearing sheep, re-routing the water courses to take away their sewage. The visitors were impressed by the self-sufficiency of the monks in previous centuries.

'You never know,' they commented. 'It may come to that one day.'

The highlight was our trip to the Yorkshire Dales. We visited Gordale Scar with its gigantic stone structures and on the hills above Malham we spotted evidence of Neolithic life in the form of stone cairns, where ancient man had lived alongside woolly mammoths, using their tusks to fashion tools. The visitors were curious and wanted to know why these ancient people had preferred to live up on the rock terraces rather than down in the valley.

'It must have been warmer on the hills then,' I said, guessing. 'I expect it was to avoid the retreating ice flows.'

'So, the climate was different then,' they said.

I was surprised they hadn't realised that.

Their visit coincided with the American elections. They joined me in watching some of the coverage on television. It was the usual story. The two rival candidates were slogging it out, taking chunks out of each other.

'The stakes are high,' I explained. 'They are fighting over who will be the next leader of the free world.'

'Why do they call it free? And why can't they decide by consensus, like we do?' One of them asked.

'I suppose it's just human nature to want to be top dog,' I said.

'Hasn't that sort of behaviour been consigned to the animal kingdom yet?' the other one said.

'Unfortunately, not,' I said. I felt myself getting defensive although there really was nothing to defend. It was despicable behaviour.

'One of the candidates thinks global warming is a Chinese hoax. He says is going to reverse all previous policies. Is that wise when it will lead inevitably to the extinction of life? What exactly is his appeal?' they asked.

I wondered where they had been for the past year and a half. It was all anyone had been talking about. I said that his appeal lay with people who felt left behind, people who had worked in coal mining and steel production in what they called the rustbelt. Their jobs had disappeared due to global capitalism because those industries had moved to other countries where the labour was cheaper. The previous government hadn't been paying enough attention to them so now they wanted to change the government.

The visitors looked disconcerted, as if they were hearing it all for the first time.

'But it's a global phenomenon,' I said, 'this shift to the right. We had it here first, with Brexit.'

They stared at me as if they didn't seem to know what I was talking about. I wondered where they had been all their lives.

'But can't people see that nations of the world

need to work together and forge common policies,' they said. 'That that it is their only hope, if they are not to destroy each other.'

They were getting agitated. I hadn't noticed it before but when I looked at them this time, they had a glazed, transparent quality. It was otherworldly. I put it down to tiredness. It was clearly time for bed.

'Our work is done here,' they said, as they left the next day. I couldn't understand why they had left so quickly. Then a letter came and everything fell into place. They thanked me for my hospitality. They explained they came from a planet in a far-away galaxy. They had used up its resources and the planet was fast becoming uninhabitable. They were on a mission to explore the possibility of re-settlement elsewhere. Earth had appealed to them at first but when faced with this new reality, they had changed their minds. They were sorry but they couldn't stay.

At this very minute, they will be hot-footing it to some other planet. I wait with trepidation for my next visitors to come.

About the author
Jenny Palmer has self-published two memoirs and a family history book, and is currently working on a collection of short stories.

Dinner for One

Robin Wrigley

Champagne

Glove between his teeth, James fumbled with his door key while trying not to lose his grip on the Tesco 'Bag for Life'. The blasted key fought against going home. The phone continued to ring. He was very close to tears.

By the time he managed to turn the key and squeeze past the artificial Christmas tree the phone had stopped ringing. He put the 'special offer' of champagne and truffles in the fridge, checked the turkey crown in the oven then switched on the answer machine.

Angela's voice crackled, 'Sorry love 'fraid I can't make it.'

Not another year!

About the author
Robin is a member of the Wimborne Writers' Group where he has been attending for the last three years. His background is that of a topographical surveyor and oil exploration country manager working worldwide.

139

Index Of Drinks

Writing For CaféLit

Have you got a story in you? Do you think it would suit CaféLit?

We're looking for thought-provoking and entertaining stories, though ones which might be a tad different from what you normally read in a woman's magazine. They should be the sort of length that would make easy reading whilst you drink a cup of coffee, even if you linger a while, but without you needing to rent a table.

So, perhaps, no more than 3000 words. Shorter stories and flash fiction are naturally very welcome.

We'll read your story. If we like it, we'll let you know and if we don't like it we'll let you know – within a month. We will work on editing with you.

Each year we'll publish a volume of the best stories. If you are in the volume you will have a share of the profits.

Our editing process will also include some work on your bio to maximise its effect.

We also ask you assign your story the name of a drink. Something light and frothy might be a hot chocolate. A dark piece of flash fiction could be an espresso. Something good for the soul would be a mint tea.

Full submission details can be found at www.cafelit.co.uk/index.php/submission-guidelines-2.

Also By Chapeltown Books

The Best of CaféLit 3, 4 and 5

Each story in these little volumes is the right length and quality for enjoying as you sip the assigned drink in your favourite Creative Café. You need never feel alone again in a café. So what's the mood today? Espresso? Earl Grey tea? Hot chocolate with marshmallows? You'll find most drinks in our drinks index.

If you're reading the café's copy and you have your Kindle or iPhone with you, why not download the Kindle version? Or browse the CaféLit web site for more examples of CaféLit stories?

www.cafelit.co.uk

Order from http://chapeltownbooks.co.uk

CaféLit 3 ISBN: 978-1-910542-00-2 (paperback)
978-1-910542-01-9 (ebook)

CaféLit 4 ISBN: 978-1-910542-02-6 (paperback)
978-1-910542-03-3 (ebook)

CaféLit 5 ISBN: 978-1-910542-04-0 (paperback)
978-1-910542-05-7 (ebook)

Chapeltown Books

Flash Collections

From Light to Dark and Back Again

by Allison Symes

This is a collection of flash fiction pieces. The tones vary from humorous to dark and back again but all reflect Allison's style of fiction. Some have appeared on Cafélit (http://cafelit.co.uk) and others on Shortbread Short Stories. The latter are some of the very first pieces she wrote years ago, CaféLit is more recent, and other stories are brand new for this collection.

"This is a quirky collection of flash fiction: from malevolent fairies to gritty contemporary dramas and bite-size funny stories. I like the way Allison is playful with words and gives a fresh slant to traditional tales. A very enjoyable read."
(Amazon)

Order from http://chapeltownbooks.co.uk

ISBN: 978-1-910542-06-4 (paperback)
978-1-910542-07-1 (ebook)

Chapeltown Books

January Stones

by Gill James

These stories were written one a day throughout January 2013. They were originally published on a blog called Gill's January Stones. Sometimes the stories would come right at the beginning of the day. Sometimes they would take a while longer.

Do they have a theme? Not really, though the idea of 'stones' is one of turning them over slowly on the beach until we find the right one.

There was no strict word count. Each story is as long as it needs to be. It had to be finished, though, by midnight of that day.

January Stones 2013
by Gill James

"The book is a quirky, easy read and most entertaining. Some of the stories make your blood run cold, others amuse, others are interesting character studies. If you want something a little bit different, this is a great place to start."
(Amazon)

Order from http://chapeltownbooks.co.uk

ISBN: 978-1-910542-10-1 (paperback)
978-1-910542-11-8 (ebook)

Chapeltown Books

Fog Lane

by Neil Campbell

Fog Lane is a collection of stories about memory. Many of the stories have been published online and in magazines. They were written over a long period of time. The oldest, *The Rose Garden* was first written in about 2007 and published in Orbis. The last one in the book, *Here Comes the Sun*, was completed in 2017. The stories in this book vary from the humorous to the sad to the macabre. They are all short stories of under a thousand words.

Order from http://chapeltownbooks.co.uk

ISBN: 978-1-910542-08-8 (paperback)
978-1-910542-09-5 (ebook)

Chapeltown Books

Spectrum

by Christopher Bowles

A collection of one hundred and ten pieces of flash-fiction and poetry. You probably won't like all of them, and some of them might even disgust you, or make you uncomfortable. But stick with it. Look at overarching themes within each coloured block. Find the puns in certain titles. Research the colours that you've never heard of. Try and work out which stories are complete fabrications, which ones contain nuggets of truth, and which ones are versions of real life events.

Order from http://chapeltownbooks.co.uk

ISBN: 978-1-910542-13-2 (paperback)
978-1-910542-14-9 (ebook)

Chapeltown Books

Our first children's picture book
of which we're immensely proud

Who Will Be My Friend?

by Colin Wyatt

'Who Will Be My Friend?' is a story about friendship, aimed at children approximately three to eight years of age. It features a Baby Bunny who is lonely and is looking for a friend to play with. Although the bunny meets lots of other animals, because of their differences they give him reasons why they can't become his friend. Finally however, Baby Bunny does succeed and finds a friend to play with and is never lonely again.

Order from http://chapeltownbooks.co.uk

ISBN: 978-1-910542-12-5 (paperback)

Chapeltown Books

www.ingramcontent.com/pod-product-compliance
Lightning Source LLC
Chambersburg PA
CBHW071304130626
46556CB00003B/1464

* 9 7 8 1 9 1 0 5 4 2 1 7 0 *